Twist of the Tongue
by
Thomas J. Farren, Sr.

D1303270

Twist of the Tongue

All Rights Reserved
© 2011 Thomas J. Farren, Sr.

For information or to order books:
L.E.A.
618 Louise Road
Glenside, PA 19038

www.language-enrichment.org

Author Page: Thomas J. Farren, Sr.

Dedication

To my wife, Alicia.

Acknowledgements

First, I want to thank my mom and dad for making the sacrifices to allow me and my siblings to have the lives we have had. You have been, and continue to be, amazing role models.

To my wife Alicia, thank you for everything, you make me smile every morning and all day. I love you.

To my children, every moment with you reminds me of the joy life can bring.

To my friends who supported me along the way in writing this I am deeply indebted. I especially want to thank Sean P. and Joe C. for the invaluable editing and proofing of early drafts. Suggestions and corrections were often eye opening. Thank you.

If I missed anyone here, I apologize. That possible oversight, as well as any errors in the book, are completely my own fault.

Note to the Reader

The story herein takes place in several different countries; for authenticity, foreign language vocabulary has been used. Every effort was made to incorporate context into usage in order both to enhance the story and to facilitate comprehension. However, there is a glossary at the end of the book which explains all terms. Any errors are attributable to the author.

Chapter One: The Letter
Bend, Oregon, USA

Getting a package at 6 a.m. had to be some kind of sick joke, thought Janey. Who the hell would pay extra for that delivery time? Annoyed, Janey rolled out of bed and went downstairs to meet the delivery man. She signed and closed the door without even looking at the thing. She could make the package wait for a little bit, even if the delivery man could not. Into the kitchen, she made a pot of fresh coffee, threw the package on the counter and started to make breakfast.

Upstairs, Rob was just beginning to wake up. Friday morning at 6:05 am, his first day off in four months, and he was awake. Great. Just how he wanted to start the day. He sat up and rolled his eyes, listening as the brown truck rolled away from the driveway. No big deal, whatever it was could wait until Monday. He jumped out of bed and walked to the bathroom for a shower. His big question for the day was whether or not to shave. He hated it. It always left his neck red and sore, and he always, always, cut himself at least once. Normally, on a day off he would ask his wife to shave his face – she had a much softer touch – but since she was downstairs, he decided to go gruff.

As he walked downstairs after the shower, the smell of French toast wafted to his nose. Umm, that smells delicious. He walked into the kitchen and stopped, admiring his wife at the stove, in a short little robe that showed off her shapely legs. Damn, he was lucky. She had to go into work today for a few hours, a half day, which left just enough time for him to run to the store to prepare a romantic little dinner.

"Who's the package for?" he asked, walking towards the counter.

"I have no idea," she replied. "It's too early to read anything but the comics."

Rob walked over to the counter and looked at the package. More of a letter, really, he thought, as he looked for the return address. Egyptian postmark? Who did they know who lived in Egypt? No return address, just the letters "JTP" scrawled across the lower left hand corner.

"Hon, do we know anyone in Egypt? Or anyone named JTP?"

She turned to him. "I don't know anyone who has even ever been to Egypt, let alone someone who lives there now. And I'm pretty sure I don't know any JTP." She turned back and faced the stove, hiding the fact that she had just lied to her husband, the first lie of their two year marriage. How could she tell him about JTP? And what the hell did he want, anyway, writing to her out of the blue with no contact in over four years? Who did he think he was?

She knew she could not give in and tear open the package. She had to wait until she was leaving for work. "Leave it there, it might be something from work. Now that I think about it, Little Benny was trying to find a pen-pal partner school for the class. I told him he could use this address. I'll check it before I leave for work."

She was not sure why she felt flustered; she had not felt anything in years for JTP. Yet, as Rob came over to kiss her neck, all she could think of was him.

===

Chapter Two: Ink
A small house in a desert

Not even sure why he was trying, JT mashed together some dirt, some saliva, and a little blood in a small concave rock. While it may have been the hundredth time he had done it, he felt like he had been doing it his whole life. He wished he had learned how to do this properly from a textbook or a lecture, how to figure out the elements to make ink, paper and glue. The sad truth was that, despite his education, he had remembered how to do this from old spy movies he watched with his dad. Even as he made this fresh well of ink, he was recalling those Sunday mornings after breakfast, watching the Three Stooges, and then at least two spy movies. He knew he had been here for over a year, the guard made sure to tell him that what seemed like months ago. Laughing and clapping, a lit cigarette on top of his bread ration his version of a joke. Happy Birthday, nameless prisoner. Over that time he had learned some of the language, Arabic. When this guard was just starting here, the previous captain had been humane to JT. He took time to speak to him and help him pronounce some words. He was by no means fluent or literate, but he could communicate, and express himself in Arabic. Fortunately for him, the guard had been careful to keep the lessons secret. JT did not know why he had been so nice to him, but when he came by to say he was being transferred, he feared he had been discovered "sharing secrets" with the enemy. But, since the other guards had made no mention of anything since his departure, JT figured he was safe.

They called him "*fil beyt*", or "in the house". It was some kind of play on the fact that this prison was an old house. JT had refused to give his real name, or any name at all for that matter. In the beginning, the interrogators told him if he cooperated, he could go home. The first guard warned, don't do it. Not only would they not let him go, they would kill him as soon as they had exhausted what they thought was all the information. If he held his silence, they would hold him indefinitely until he decided to talk. "Your government can find you if you are alive, but not if you are dead," he had said to JT. If only he knew; JT was already dead to his government. When he had signed on for this mission, he agreed to cut all communications to his life. If he was successful, he could go back, say he had tried out for a special ops team. If he failed, well, he failed.

As he wrote now, he was not even sure to whom he should address it. Or if it would ever reach any destination outside this sandy hell. The boy had been bringing water since the first day, his only job and his permission to talk to soldiers. After he had learned some Arabic, JT offered to teach the boy some English. The boy was hesitant at first, then a little mistrustful; yet with each passing day JT made no request, and so gained the boy's trust. It became a respite from the day's grind for each of them. The American did not make fun of the boy for being so small and wanting to be a soldier, and the boy brought the cheerful exuberance of youth to a haggard prisoner.

When he first overheard the news, JT was not sure what to do. When he had made his decision, he

knew he had to be very careful not to scare the boy away. He had to make a few small requests, little things like smuggled cigarettes, or fresh cheese. The only gift he could offer in return was to share stories of America. With each new little gift, JT would reveal what had happened to the young car driving rebel, or who had assassinated the youthful president. But this, this which would be his last request, might be too much for the boy to do, or to even ask the boy. Time was running out, though, and so were his options.
===

Chapter Three: The Recruit
Santiago, Chile

Gerardo hated the morning commute through Santiago. Living in the Las Condes section with his uncle was a treat, but taking the microbus was not. It was usually fine when he hopped on the bus, but by the time the micro turned onto Avenida Bernardo O'Higgins, people were literally hanging out the doors. He had learned early to take a seat facing the rear door so he could push his way through. He had decided not to buy a car because of the expenses involved, and his unusual hours and job. He wanted to be able to come and go without people knowing his presence by that of his car.

This morning as he entered the bus, there was already a clown doing tricks for tips, and an ice-cream salesman pitching his wares as he ambled to the back door to jump off and onto the next micro. Having traveled abroad a few years back, Gerardo appreciated the uniqueness of what he was watching. He had never been to a place that had performers and ice-cream sellers on their buses.

He sat down and quickly put his mind to the tasks of the day. It had been some time now since they had discovered the leak. When the "student" was captured, they all heaved a sigh of relief. It was okay, they were safe. Since the capture, however, they had heard nothing. Nothing. Was he killed? Tortured? Did he give up his information?

Every event of the past 10 years came back to him in those few moments on the micro. His uncle's call seemed out of the blue. Come live with him in

Santiago? Leave his home in Puerto Montt? He went one weekend to spend time with his uncle to discuss it. His uncle was getting older, and his own children did not really talk to him. He did not want another son, nor did he want to steal Gerardo from his own parents. He wanted a connection to the youth of his country. He wanted to know what they were saying, feeling, wanting. In return, he offered Gerardo a place in his house, and the promise of his recommendation, and that of influential friends, to any university he wished to attend.

When he made the decision, his parents sat him down. They were not surprised or upset. They understood the opportunity, and the temptation, of it all. His mother held his hand as his father spoke. "Be your own man. Make your own decisions. Be able to sleep at night. Come to us if you ever need help with anything." That was it. Not unlike his father and the Germanic character of the region, but also startlingly emotional. Those few words summed up his father's decision to move the family to Puerto Montt. To change their *apellido* to de Castillo. Gerardo de Castillo. He did not at first understand the name change; only through schooling and schoolyard jokes did he learn. And now he was returning to the city abandoned by his parents. To live with his uncle.

Had he been his own man? As he checked the memories he convinced himself that yes, he had been so. His arrival into the city had been a shock, and he went on the defensive immediately. His uncle was patient and kind. Asked questions and showed interest, but never pushed him into a decision. True, he had been influenced by his uncle, by living with this man and meeting his influential friends. But he had been his own man. He was sure of it. Every letter home stated that for his parents' benefit.

===

Chapter Four: The Prince
Dublin, Ireland

James liked to whistle when he walked, usually traditional Irish tunes. He had taken to it only recently after a trip to the continent. There, he encountered in every major city the same sense of cosmopolitan malaise that he found in present day Dublin. Only 35, he felt the city of his youth was more close to that of Yeats than Bono. The city now had changed, much for the better, and as much for the worse. It was a European city, grand, bustling and ethnically diverse. But it was just that, European; it was becoming like Rome, Paris, Vienna. The sense of its character was being lost in the growth. The street bands playing mountain tunes are not so prevalent anymore; street vendors are more likely to sell t-shirts and cheap bracelets than fresh food or artwork; and more people wear Dolce & Gabana than clothes from local woolen mills.

And so James returned from the continent and started to inject a little Irish into each of his days. Just a little. Most people smiled at him knowingly, remembering the song. Some joined in with their voice or clapping. Tourists loved it. Resident aliens shot him dour glances, which made him whistle louder and stronger.

Today he was in a particularly good mood and was whistling completely for himself. It had taken him and his family fifteen years to arrange everything and gather together all the right people.

In one month, the meeting would set it out and the assignments would be made. Patience and diligence were paying off. All the invitees had agreed to come to the meeting except one, and that response was expected shortly. Transportation was all ready, accommodations were set. Even alibis were memorized in case there was a compromise. The only glitch had been some lawyers and judges who could not be bribed. They could neither be taken out of the equation due to their public stature and rank. Thankfully, new technology allowed them to be followed and marked. They would be easy to avoid.

The tricky part would be the summation, the resolve to stand together in the face of international pressure and threats. He had been working on that speech for years with his father. They rehearsed it, memorized it, put it down for a year and re-read it for weaknesses. It was a brilliant speech, one that could bring you to tears, or to arms.

===

Chapter Five: Janey
Bend, Oregon

Janey stepped out of the shower and got ready for work. Blow drying her hair and ironing her skirt, she could not stop thinking about JT. She had long since gotten over him; that was not the problem. She was happily married, had a good job and a good life. She loved being able to walk up the street, over the river bridge, and into town to work. She knew everyone and everyone knew her. The children loved her. Now, though, the pressures of the East Coast, so long removed, came flooding back to her.

Everything in DC moved so quickly, she did not know how to act differently. So she fell in love with JT. Johnboy, she liked to call him. It made him seem so dashing and courageous, yet young and innocent. They had dreamed together of the future, fighting for the right causes, not crusading, but working with confidence and a clear conscience. They did not want to "bring down" anyone or any organization; they wanted to see people – all people – work and live together, like a family. Like a family with all the love and concern, all the sibling rivalries and fights, all the make-ups and moving on, together. They would have been happy. They would have been, she thought.

Janey finished getting dressed, re-hashing in her head what had attracted her to JT, and how she had forced herself to move on with her own life.

"You want a ride to work, hon?" she heard Rob call from the bottom of the steps.

"No, I have a quick afternoon meeting before I

head home, so I'll need my car" she lied, again.
Shoot. She had to figure out what that letter said. She headed downstairs and quietly slipped the letter into her purse.

"What are you planning today with all your time off?" she asked.

"I'm hoping to call Steve and go golfing. Maybe a little racquetball, though, since he wants to try to even up our scores. Right now I'm up, eleven games to nine."

"Well, don't pull a muscle. I'll call you on the way home."

Janey pulled out of the driveway and pulled the letter out of her purse. She still had an hour before work, but said she wanted to get some work done. She headed towards work, and then a few blocks before, she parked and walked into a random coffee shop. She was moving quickly now, and had to force her foot off the gas pedal more than once on the way over here. She was shaking and she had not even had a sip of coffee yet.

She sat down at the table and suddenly froze. No shaking, no hurry, she felt calm. She opened the letter, and gasped aloud at what she pulled out. It was a ragtag collection of papers, torn clothe and what she could only assume was some kind of animal skin. The papers had writing on it, which language she could not tell, but more importantly, there was fresh writing over it. Was that? Could it be? Blood?

Out of the corner of her eye, she noticed people glancing over at her. She had been talking aloud. She wished she had chosen a corner booth, but how could she know the contents would be so shocking. As best they could, they were bound by string, in what she assumed was the proper order. Janey took a sip of coffee, and started to read the cover page:

> "Dear Janey, I know this is going to be random and scary. But you were the only one I knew I could trust. It took months to find you, but thanks to technology, even Bedouins can go online. I need you to read this all, read it and memorize it. Do not transcribe it! There's no time. If you copy them, get them away from you, to a bank deposit box, or something. Please, just trust me. If this gets denied, you know the truth, you will know what to do. There is so much I want to tell you, but cannot. These pages will serve that purpose, and others. Once you have it memorized, call Bill from college. Have him see, not read, the documents. Send them to a Dr. Ogilvie, care of Dean Bulgiuno, back at school. Janey, I may not get out of this, I may not get to explain. I picked you because when I finished this writing I had to send it to someone who would care for the truth first. I had to trust the woman I love. Ever. JT"

Love. Not used to love, loved, or loved years ago. Love, presently. Janey almost fainted. Everything came crashing back. The energy and the goals, then the abrupt abandonment and isolation. She started to well up, and quickly grabbed a handkerchief. She could not go to work, she had to tell Rob. She had to tell him, everything.

===

Chapter Six: Dinner

I need to go shopping this time of day every week, thought Rob. He was through the supermarket and liquor store in record time. He arrived home and started to prepare everything. First he put the candle upstairs, and ordered the flowers to be delivered at 5:30. Then he walked into the kitchen and did preliminary preparations for dinner.

Rob almost dropped the china when, out of the corner of his eye, he saw Janey walk through the kitchen door.

"What are you..." he stopped mid-sentence. Something was clearly wrong. She was disheveled and sobbing. He put the china down and guided Janey to the table. "What's the matter, baby? What is it? Are you okay?"

"Rob, I need to tell you something. I need you to hear it all. Now. And I'm sorry I did not tell you this when you proposed. It's about my last boyfriend, my fiancé, before you and I met."

Janey started at sophomore year, and Rob's knuckles went white.

===

Chapter Seven: The Last RSVP
Santiago, Chile

Gerardo opened his office door and sat down. It was happening. The reality of it hit him as he picked up the phone, and he had to hang it up. He had been his own man. He hated when his family had to move south. Had to leave the city. It was exciting growing up, playing soccer, talking to the traffic light jugglers, marveling at the spinning drummers in the *parques*. When he asked if he could learn to play the drum on his back and spin also, his father had been very stern, "This family does not spin for amusement and pesos. This family works for the future of the country." This family works.

Did he ever have a choice to be his own man? He had to work. He became his own man when he came back to Santiago. When he left the south. These arrangements were the culmination of his maturity.

He quietly thanked his uncle for rescuing him from ignominy. From being embarrassed of who he was. His father and his uncle disagreed, true, but his uncle never felt humiliation for what his father did. His father, rather than reciprocate, felt nothing but shame for his uncle. Yet his uncle was a great man, a man who had, in fact, worked for the good of the country and its people. In spite of everything his father did not say about his uncle, he had worked hard for the future of the country.

Even after he learned why his father did not speak of his uncle, he was unconvinced. He was old enough to know that countries do not run because people want them to do so. Countries run because strong men lead them to greatness, sometimes in the face of others, sometimes over others. Gerardo knew that one life was worth risking for a few thousand, so a few thousand were worth risking for a few million. The evidence was all around him now in the city. This city, once so proud and full of promise, was losing its luster quickly.

For years, the country had lived a quiet life, protecting itself and its possessions. The people never changed their character; they were kind, inviting and sociable. But for many years, his uncle had seen that they maintained a balance. People were home with their families every night by 10 p.m. It was safe to walk the streets. The economy was the strongest in the region.

At first, when the country was "itself" again, nothing changed much. There was almost a sigh of relief. But now, just a few short years later, the city was manifesting the changes that were slowly eating away at it. The metro, while still efficient, was dirty and grimy. Wild dogs wandered the city, dying on walkways and in parks. The wandering student poets, once limited in number, now flourished throughout the city, pestering businessmen and tourists alike.

The economy was starting to flounder and the government was being asked to stop its job in order to research the past. It was time. He could see it even before he received that first phone call a few years ago. An accent he recognized after a few minutes, and a name he knew instantly.

"Operator, I need to make an international call."

As he waited for the phone to be answered, Gerardo smiled. He knew what he was doing. He knew his uncle was proud. He knew his father would one day understand and be proud, too.

"Hello," chimed the familiar voice.

"*Ya venimos. Está listo. Ciao.*"

Simple as that.

===

Chapter Eight: Fil Beyt
A small house in a desert

For months, JT had been talking to the boy and finding out what he knew and what he could do. Technology had been changing the way of life for these people during the past few years. While the young did not know what they were missing, some of the old lamented the changes to their culture. Some welcomed them from the harshness of it all. Either way, all JT cared about was that this boy had access to a computer, and knew how to use it.

He had slowly taken months to convince the boy he was lamenting the loss of his loved ones. He guarded the names and details, revealing a new twist each time the boy's interest seemed to wane. He did it with several types of people, actually. He reminisced about his brother, his mother, even his dog. Each time, the boy shared stories of his own family, in his way trying to comfort this foreign man. When JT found out he had a crush on a local girl, he saw another opportunity, a lost love.

There had only ever been one love in his life, he highlighted to the boy. The one he left behind. The one for whom he should have left this life behind. He began to work her into the story. Each new tale brought her back fresh to his mind. Their last night together had been arranged by her as an anniversary date, two years together. She had convinced her roommate to spend the night elsewhere, convincing her that this night alone with JT would show him how much she truly loved him.

He remembered it all in that desert: the fresh flowers, the scented candles, the CD playing a mix of jazz, Barry White, and Dean Martin. He described it so well even the boy felt he had been there. But the boy was not, did not love her. JT did, still did. And he knew. She had to be the one. She would be mad, she would not understand at first, but he knew she would do the right thing. That he could count on as he had so many times when they were together.

The first time he saw Janey he knew he loved her. She did not even see JT that first day. He was walking across campus to class, head down into the wind. She was standing outside the university cafeteria with friends. It was her laugh that first attracted him. He looked up and saw a beautiful brunette, with light eyes and smile that stopped his breath from 100 feet away. He slowed his pace and walked past her and noticed some of the books spilling out of the backpack. Third level philosophy with Professor James. He had that class. He kept on smiling and waited just outside the classroom, stealthily entering after her. He took the seat next to her and pretended not to notice. Without the hat, she would have felt unnerved by this guy staring at her. It was not until she passed him the course expectation sheet that she even noticed him. Looking back, it's safe to say she was not as quickly enamored. But she did notice him; he needed to lose the hat. It made him look 12. It also piqued her interest; what was under that hat? So it was that she said yes to a date when he finally asked at the end of the last class. That's how he won her over.

JT chuckled to himself about that first date, even now in the pits of hell. He looked at the boy and knew he was hooked. He knew that if he finished this whole story without losing control of his own emotions, the boy would help him.

What was he thinking then? asked the boy.

Well, JT explained, he wanted a great first date, one that would knock her off her feet. He grabbed his housemates and asked for ideas. Bobby gave him an idea from one of his buddies from his old neighborhood in Philly. It sounded nuts, but it also sounded unique, and JT, and everyone else in the house, wanted in on it. James and Michael bought the fruit, wine, cheese and Tupperware, while Bobby, Brian and JT scouted out locations on campus. It took all afternoon, and two cut classes, but they found a little niche in the middle of campus, and it was just what they hoped for.

JT told Janey it would be a late night and he would pick her up at 11:30. A little confused, she agreed. All night the guys cut up berries, picked a CD for the portable player – Dean Martin, and packed it all into a backpack. JT walked down to the spot and started to spread out the blanket. By 11:15 he was ready and went for Janey.

"What is it that has you so crazy for this girl from your village?" JT asked.

"She is nice to me, she holds my hand and she listens to my stories" the boy replied. "Even when others leave me alone."

"That's the same for my Janey. She was nice to me, and she let me take her on this date. She was not afraid to hold my hand, either."

She should have that first night; most other girls would have. He picked her up and walked her the long way down, past the school buildings and the front plaza. Coming down the steps, all one could see were trees and beyond that the playing fields. To the right was a school building, to the left, the university cemetery for deceased priests. JT turned.

"Why are you turning left" Janey asked, feet planted on the bottom step.

"Do you believe I won't lie to you?" replied JT.

"Should I?"

"Yes, you should. I won't ever lie to you, and you'll see that if you believe me now."

"So, Mr. Truth, why are you turning left?"

Damn, cute and sassy. "I thought you might like some fruit."

Janey turned, then looked JT in the eyes. She smiled and grabbed JT's hand, trusting him. They walked along the outer edge of the cemetery, along the line of trees and almost imperceptibly, Dean floated to their ears, flickering along with the candle lights. Janey planted her feet again, but this time with her mouth open and her eyes wide. In front of her, at the foot of the trees in front of the cemetery, she saw a complete picnic layout: thick blanket; various bowls of strawberries, cherries, grapes, mangos and kiwi; candles; a wine bottle and two glasses; and a CD player. She was hooked.

"We talked until the sun came up. We ate every piece of fruit, listened to that music until we sang the words and we held hands all night."

"Was that because she was afraid of the dead people?"

"Probably, but I didn't care. I don't care. It was an amazing night. Nobody in the house could believe I had pulled it off. It seemed to strange. Janey loved it. It was simple, pure, a night for the two of us under trees in a calm, serene atmosphere."

Wanting to ask the boy then, JT was overcome and had to stand up. Damn, he had no idea he could still taste those strawberries in the desert. As he composed himself, he thought he missed his chance. He turned around, and the boy was staring at him, with big, pensive brown eyes peering into his soul.

"You miss her, yes? You would like to see her again?"

"More than anything."

And the boy took off. Well, JT realized, at least he would die with a happy thought in his head.

===

Chapter Nine: The Beginning for JT
Sophomore Summer

Coming back to campus as a junior, JT was not the same man. He had spent most of freshman year unsure of what he was doing, or why he was even in school. He often thought he should have stayed on at the construction site. He was earning good money there, was outside, and could talk as little or as much as he wanted. He plodded through freshman year, however, always reassuring himself that this would open more opportunities, whatever they were. He was convinced he'd finish the year that way, until one of his friends suggested he try out for the baseball team. JT only played two years in high school, but he loved the game. He would watch games and shout at the TV, he would quote random stats at the dinner table, and, much to his roommates' delight, would win trivia bets at parties. It took several suggestions, but JT finally decided to give it a whirl. Worst case scenario was that he would continue on as he thought he would anyway. If he made the team, he'd get to play ball. That was worth the risk. And, much to his surprise, he made the team. That made his freshman year. He was a little quiet at first, but soon enough, he mingled with his new teammates, came to know the coaches and trainers, and dove headfirst back into the game. Sure enough, he was happier, his focus was improved, and he was exercising. Most importantly, he knew he could do well.

Going home for the summer to Philadelphia after freshman year, he was excited. He was ending school on a good note. Going home was going to be a fun time, though. He could not wait to get back to work and catch up with the crew. His friends were all coming home, also, from their respective colleges.

And now that he could afford to pay for his car insurance, he was allowed to drive the family car. JT thought nothing could make this summer bad. And he was correct. He had a great summer, made good money and entered sophomore year confident as ever. Everything went well for JT that year. That was the year he got serious with Janey. He was able to woo her freshman year, but sophomore year was the year he fell in love with her. As the academic year wound to a close, JT went into that summer with the same high expectations as last. This time, though, he was hoping to buy a car so he could go visit Janey, maybe hit the beach for a few weeks. Even better, he knew that this summer at work, he would no longer be bottom man on the totem pole. There would be a freshman, or a recent high school grad just starting out. And next year on the baseball team, he had a good shot at making starting Varsity. JT could not have been happier heading into summer before junior year.

Two weeks into the vacation, JT's dad was involved in a car accident on the Turnpike. It was a nasty accident that was caused by some guy screaming at his secretary on his cell phone. He rear-ended some other guy in an SUV who was trying to read the sports page on the passenger seat.

As the second guy turned the wheel on braking, he turned into the lane where JT's dad was idling in a small hold-up on the turnpike. When the SUV turned, it rolled sideways and flipped, rolling twice before finally landing on top of the small Escort, and on Mr. Parral. He was killed instantly, the other two walked away unharmed.

The accident took everyone by surprise, and Mrs. Parral did not handle it well. An only child, with aging parents, she felt alone. JT could say or do nothing to help her. She was frozen. JT had to take care of all the arrangements, and he grew up. He learned more than he wanted to know about how to bury a family member. Sitting in church, listening to the priest drone on about the will of God, JT just stared at his mom. She just stared.

JT knew he had the support of his friends, the support of Janey, but he felt alone at home. Janey could not stay all summer; her parents weren't thrilled that she had stayed for two weeks. When she left, it was JT and his mom; his mom who barely spoke, barely ate, barely moved. Her skin became pale, her eyes became hollow and her hair started to fall out. The family doctor came to visit, the priest, even her best friends, but nothing made a dent on her.

As the teenage son took over all the responsibilities of the house, the mother continued to regress into a childlike, helpless, state. The entire time, JT tried to pray. He took out his rosary and recited twice daily. He knelt every night before bed to plead with God, just for relief. It did not come. By the summer's end, Mrs. Parral was taken to the hospital and referred to a clinic. JT had to sell the house or drop out of school. It was all happening so fast, he did not know what to do. So he called his baseball coach. Coach Sullivan drove up and took him to talk. Walking along Kelly Drive, JT said little, but listened. Not realizing the reason, he agreed to come back to school, agreed to stay on the team. He agreed to it all only because coach was an adult figure to him. In that one day, the coach had taken on an air of father figure for JT.

The school offered free tuition for JT for a year, and, if he made the baseball team again, the coach promised to go to bat for him for an athletic scholarship for his final year. JT went back, and wrote a letter a day to his mom. He was positive in each letter, sometimes fibbing that he had aced an exam, or met some star speaker on campus, all in attempts to make his mom smile. He told stories about Janey, hoping in some way she would get to know the girl he loved. He still prayed, but every prayer felt more hollow as every day passed without a return letter. When his mom died in early December, JT barely registered it.

He touched base with the doctor once a week and he knew it was coming. He knew he could not stop it, in spite of everything. His lack of sadness left a hole in him, a hole which was filled with anger. His rage was directed against God because He could stop it, and did not. His anger was inflamed when he went back to Philadelphia to arrange everything for his mom. As he was sorting through her belongings in the clinic, he found his letters, in a pile on the bureau, unopened. Not a single one was opened, almost seventy letters. Not a single person in the clinic bothered to even read them to her. His mom had suffered those last months without her son, without even the smallest hope that he was doing well. He had suffered every day, waiting for a letter, a postcard, a phone call. Nothing ever arrived. And God had let it happen. Well, thought JT, then I can happen without God. And he stopped praying.

That Christmas, instead of celebrating anything, JT packed up and went camping. Janey was upset, thought he should not be alone, but she knew she could not force him to come to her house to celebrate. That would only push him away. She would be there when he returned. He drove to the Poconos and set up camp in an isolated location. He went hiking, he walked, he slept, he cried, he shouted. After a week, when he thought it was out of his system, he sat down and set up rules for himself. He was alone, so he had to depend on himself. He was determined to succeed, to live the life that was robbed from him and his family.

He would live. As he sat there on the last day of camping, alone in the woods, he felt almost hopeless. He felt positive about his resolutions, but he knew they were simple and vague. He needed some kind of direction. Something to kick him into gear. The realization that he could not provide that impetus stung him, and brought with it melancholy. JT returned to school, reliving his freshman year mode.

Coach noticed it right away, and had the players spend extra, though subtle, attention to JT. He asked around about JT's classes and his friends. He remembered back to JT's try-outs for the team.

Although at first a little annoyed when JT tried out as the only un-recruited player, he was taken by his determination. As he brought the team into the new season, he could see JT was missing that. He looked like a freshman again. He knew if he did nothing, not only might JT never succeed in baseball, he might never succeed in life. Through all the questioning, the one common thread coach found was languages. In high school, JT had Italian and Greek, and in college was trying on Spanish.

When he called JT in for a meeting, he had already spoken to the Dean about the possibilities. It took some cajoling, but the Dean would permit JT to study in Latin America to perfect his Spanish. As a requirement for going, he would have to agree to an International Business minor. So, Coach talked to him and persuaded him that he needed a change of pace, a change of life, if only temporarily. JT went to speak with the Dean.

===

Chapter Ten: The Dean
Washington, DC

Dean Anthony Bulgiuno had been Dean of the Business School for close to twelve years. In a city like D.C., that can lead to a good number of high level connections. He was savvy enough to develop those connections, and comfortable enough to not use them. This had built his reputation as a man who could be trusted without needing to be compensated. This in turn had helped raise his stature within the beltway. Even he, however, was a little surprised when he was approached by Agent Chris Grelsh.

Agent Grelsh had been in Washington for years, and had heard many good things about this dean. After watching him, and checking his records, he knew this was an opportunity. The dean in a major university, with exposure to thousands of young intelligent adults, was something he could not ignore. Moreover, it was a university which prided itself on its international character. He wanted the dean simply to keep an eye out for potential recruits. Grelsh was working through the CIA to keep tabs on the world's leaders. Clearly, he could not be everywhere, but the right people with the right equipment, could make it seem like he was. The dean could help him find those people.

When Coach Sullivan had spoken to him, and explained the situation of this sophomore, Bulgiuno had to pay attention. This kid was loose, capable, athletic, and, whether he knew it or not, open to suggestion. He had already spoken to Grelsh, and he agreed to feel him out, see what was there.

This was a chance to make another connection, with possible beneficial long term results. So Bulgiuno watched as JT walked across the quad to his office, and noticed everything. Without a hesitation in his step, yet with fluidity, this kid just blended in to the scenery. People barely gave him a second glance, let alone get out of his way. He did not even have to open the door to the building, just slipped in behind the closing door. Not bad.

"Hi. My name is JT Parral. I have a 12:30 appointment with the Dean."

"Just have a seat, son" said the secretary, "He'll be with you in a moment."

JT picked up a newspaper as he sat down to wait. He was not really sure why. He never read when he waited. He liked to watch the people come and go. When the door to the office creaked open, his eyes had been on it for over a minute.

"Good afternoon, JT, my name is Anthony Bulgiuno. Coach Sullivan had some nice things to say about you."

"Thank you, sir. That's very nice of you to say."

Thus began the 45 minute meeting in which the dean learned much about JT. It was his trip to Italy as an Italian language student which cemented his love of travel, and meeting new people, and learning new languages. He was very appreciative of this chance to go to Chile to perfect his Spanish, and he knew that he would make the dean proud to have sent him. The dean also learned that JT wanted to travel to the Middle East to do some amateur archaeology because of his studies with Ancient Greek.

It was a fact which meant little to Bulgiuno, but perked up the ears of Grelsh when he heard of it later. That was a tidbit to hold onto.

"Well, JT, things look pretty good on this end. There is just one thing we need to do before we can give you the green light on this study abroad."

Still a little indifferent, though interested, JT asked, "And what would that be, sir?"

Dean Bulgiuno paused, looked down at the desk and bit his lip. He needed JT to go along with this; he could not mess this part up. "Well, son", he paused and glanced at JT, whose eyes caught the word, "we're worried about you. We know that it has been, well, that life has been difficult recently. We don't want to send you around the world without support. We want to make sure you can handle being uprooted from your environment, your classes, your roommates. There is a school specialist you will have to speak to, a Dr. Ogilvie, who will help you sort out what might happen when you travel overseas. It'll just give you a heads up on what you might expect. Are you agreed to do that?"

JT sat there quietly, pondering. If he went overseas, he might have a chance to think, to figure out if what he was doing was what he wanted to be doing. "Yeah, uh, I mean, yes. I can do that."

"Good. Be here tomorrow at nine sharp. We'll use this office. See you then."

As soon as JT left, Bulgiuno called Grelsh. Dr. Ogilvie had a client.

===

Chapter Eleven: Janey and JT
Bend, Oregon

Rob was angry; no, Rob was pissed. He knew nothing of Janey's fiancé; he knew nothing because she never mentioned him before. Here she was telling him that she just received a package with letters - written in blood! - from him, sent from some desert in Egypt. He listened calmly at first, understood that they were college sweethearts. He understood that they grew closer due to the tragedies in his life. He had to ask again, though, about what happened when JT and Janey returned to school. How did this guy go from college sweetheart to fiancé to ghost?

"It was a natural consequence," said Janey. "He had lost just about everything he knew, his parents, his house. He lost the life he knew, and he was not sure how to continue. One night we sat down and talked about what he was feeling, what he was thinking. Before we had met, I was doing some volunteer work. I was able to talk him into coming with me a few times. He really made a big impression on the people there. The people who worked there took to him quickly. And the people we helped, well, they related to him. They did not see anything other than JT. He responded to it.

So, when we sat down to talk, we realized that our time working together had given some direction to his life. Before his life was changed. He wanted to hold onto that. I wanted him to hold onto that. We made a decision to more heavily invest ourselves. We chose two organizations we thought could use some help and offered our time. Being in D.C., we had the opportunity to effect change all around the country.

We knew if we could begin to have congressmen start talking about the issues back in their home states, there was a possibility, at least, that the conversation would extend to the floor of Congress. It was a long shot, but we were young, we were passionate…"

"Just how passionate?" interrupted Rob.

"We were passionate about our *work*. And yes, it brought us closer, faster than it would have otherwise. We thought we could make a change, together."

"And then he just left? That doesn't make any sense." Rob was watching Janey, even as he paced. Janey shook her head.

"Exactly. He was having a tough time, obviously. But, I was always there for him. His coach was talking to him. His teammates always had an eye out for him. When he came to see me about studying abroad, I was a little hesitant. I was. I was afraid on so many levels. I thought I could lose him. I thought our work would slowly fade and that would mean our connection would fade. I thought he might not want to see me when he came back because I would be too boring. But JT kept reassuring me that he would never leave me, that he would never stop loving me. I wanted to show him, um…"

Damn, thought Janey, how could she word this?

"I wanted to show him how much he meant to me. I convinced my roommate to go out for the night. I bought some of the same CD's from our first date, had flowers and candles, I even cooked dinner. I was trying to surprise him because I told him I wanted to go to a movie. And he was surprised. But, even more,

he surprised me. After desert, he cleared the table
left just the candle and the flowers. Then he dropped
on one knee, and, well, he proposed. Said he could
never love another. That I was his world. We spent
the night talking and he thanked me for
understanding."

Tears streaming down her eyes, Rob sat down
and put an arm around her. This was not necessarily
the time to act macho and jealous.

"It's okay, baby. Keep going. What happened
next?"

"Then he left in early summer for orientation in
Chile. They had a few weeks to get situated and meet
their host families. We wrote letters every week. We
talked on the phone every other night. About three
months into his time there, he started cutting our
conversations short. His letters started to get cryptic,
like he was afraid of something. I was a little worried,
but, I did not know any better. I just thought it was
part of the experience; that he was having fun and
maybe, just maybe, getting to his old self again. I was
petrified that my worst fears were being realized, yet I
was almost happy, if that makes sense. Then I
received a letter ending our communication, and I
freaked out.

I finally found his advisor and talked to him,
and he convinced me it was best to let JT figure out
who he was. Besides, he was flying home at the end
of November. I even booked the flight for him. I
figured whatever it was would go away when he came
home."

As Janey took a deep breath, Rob clenched his
jaw and waited.

ver did. I sat in the airport for hours
ed. I thought he was held up in
gage was lost, or something. But
never called. He never wrote. I
w where he was or where he's been."

Janey looked at Rob. "I have not heard from
him until I received that letter. It took me over a year
to accept what happened. I went through all kinds of
stories. I thought, maybe, maybe he abandoned me.
Maybe he was in some prison. Maybe there was an
accident. But no matter what I created, it eventually
came down to me having to accept that he was not
coming back. And I did. I moved on, and I decided to
leave him as abruptly as he left me. I moved here to
get a fresh start."

Janey smiled and let out a soft laugh, eased her
shoulders, and looked Rob in the eyes. "And that's
when I met you."

===

Chapter Twelve: A New San Martín
Santiago, Chile

Gerardo hung up the phone and lit a cigar. Contemplating the phone call, history came rushing to him. He and his uncle were on the forefront of a new revolution. More than that, a new style of revolution. When the Americans fought for their freedom, they had leaders like Jefferson and Washington. They were, in fact, revolutionaries for their time. Concepts taken for granted the world over – equality, justice, liberty – were still just nascent ideas in the late 18th century. Their rebellion against England sparked movements elsewhere in the world, both in the New World and the Old. For more than 200 years their ideas raged and took over the world.

Gerardo sat back and looked at the headlines of the paper, a trick his uncle taught him. If you had no time to read the article, the headline would at least clue one in to what was happening. Now, Gerardo saw nothing but worldwide problems of violence, war, crime and poverty. All of this was present after 200 hundred years of "equality, justice, liberty". Gerardo snorted a laugh.

Chile was a great test Gerardo knew the group never could have planned. The recent history of the country, from the rise and fall of the dictatorship, to the growing economic success, taught lessons that no text could. In the 1960's, the Christian Democrats came to power by winning over the middle and working classes.

They were ousted from power, however, by the military and the land owning class, who, despite historical superiority, suddenly felt underappreciated. The success of the dictatorship was doomed in the plebiscite of 1988 not because it lacked success, but because, as the then-mayor of Copiapó stated, the people "have to feel they are participating."

Even his uncle explained for him the benefit of life after the dictatorship, the benefit of hindsight. People did not need to have great lives, people did not even have to "move up" in the social order. They simply needed to feel that their voice was heard and they had an impact on their country. That momentary sensation shifted their thought process and they began to believe their resultant life was better, whether or not it actually changed. It was a startling revelation, one that seemed so simple, yet had proven so elusive to hundreds and thousands of politicians and leaders.

Very few countries in the history of the world had a single, continuous style of government for more than a few hundred years. Arguably the USA was the most successful, with ancient Rome providing a model, as well. But in looking at both, glaring problems emerge. For the last 200 years of the Roman Empire through the second to fourth centuries, once the Germans tribes crossed the Danube River, the empire was constantly besieged by attacks.

The Romans went from an offensive might to a defensive power. The United States, while maintaining itself as the greatest economic power in the world, had problems of inequality and poverty on a level with sub-Saharan Africa. That no one mentions the problems does not erase them. Gerardo knew all this, and knowing this, he listened intently to his uncle explain the method.

Every revolution in history, whether successful or not, was a failure. The true goals were never achieved, men were never equal, nor even had equal access to achievement. Old money and old power were old for a reason. Those people had learned how to weather the tides of humanity. As such, the true powers behind the government always measured every step they took. Nothing was left to chance or luck. They thrived on anonymity from the masses. They never let their names be published in any Forbes list of "richest" people. Should their friends fall into risk of being arrested, they were ushered away for several years until the memory of their actions were mollified by the forgetfulness of time. Gerardo absorbed it all in as his uncle continued on explaining that most Americans don't care, let alone even realize, that their "Founding Fathers" held slaves and punished free-speaking journalists, both anathema to the very principles they espoused for the young colonies. Even in their own Latin American continent, both José de San Martín and Simón Bolívar were considered heroes, despite their heated differences, fractious politicking and violent outbursts.

"It has always been so," concluded his uncle, "and it will always be so because people do not have the luxury of reflection when they have the necessity of hunger."

Gerardo smiled as he remembered the naïveté of his next question. "Uncle, how can we ever hope to change that?"

The basic truth was that every revolution always looked at the issue as two sides, as a winner and a loser. The rich were always targeted, and the poor always did the targeting. Therefore, the rich had things taken away from them, and the poor, ostensibly anyway, had those things handed over to them.

"But," interrupted Gerardo, "we know that. If all revolutions essentially fail because the powerful know ways to maintain their power and wealth despite any façade of a *coup*, and the poor eventually revert to focusing on living, what will this revolution accomplish?"

"*Mi sobrino*, what did we learn from Chile?"

"Well, the people wanted to be a part of their government. They wanted to feel that their voice was heard."

"Correct. And what have we seen in the United States, the supposed best example of a 'voice of the people government'?"

"We have seen the lowest voter turnout in a democracy in history because the people feel that their votes do not matter. As a result, those who do vote wield some power, but those in power feel no obligation to anyone, either those that vote or those who do not. All of this has led to a country in which the people are given money through a complex system of social welfare to keep them quiet. The poor receive a little money for food, clothes, and bills; the rich receive corporate bailouts and lucrative government contracts; and nothing of substance changes."

"*Eso es*," said his uncle. "Nothing of substance changes. Even in Puerto Rico, a commonwealth of the USA, where the voter turnout is one of the highest in the world because the people want to control their own destiny, there are no changes. Simply put, it is because they are but one small part in the giant that is the US Government. They remain as the last colony in the Western hemisphere because the only voice that matters cares not for them. That is not just. The people at the top become richer, those at the bottom are psychologically beaten into submission, and those in the middle are fooled into thinking they can become the top. They give money to the rich, they give subsistence to the poor, and they give false hope to the middle. They themselves do this without thinking because they have been trained. However, the times of achieving their goals, of working towards a better life, are gone. They are robbed by being supplied. The problem, then, is no one feels they have earned anything. They, oddly enough, feel they are entitled to everything. The actions we are taking will curb this, especially the influence it is exerting worldwide by means of the popularity of American culture."

"And we will make this better, uncle?"

"Yes! We will make this better because we will no longer permit this spectacle to continue. In our revolution, we will unite. We will bring all of Latin America into one house. In our new revolution, we will not take anything from the rich, we will not give anything to the poor. We will not use *nuestros hermanos puertorriqueños* for their land or their sugar. We will give them the outcome of their votes and not take over their lives. Like José de San Martín – who turned down titles and honors to fight for his cherished countrymen – we will fight for the unity of Latin America. We will offer the people their rightful inheritance. We will offer a true, achievable manner in which to live. However, in order to be in our society, one must be of the society. Only those who work, in some manner, will be able to see a life well lived. Our role is not to control their lives, but, in the true sense of the word, to manipulate them. We will help them see what they can become, what they can achieve, and how they can contribute to the collective good. This can not be done if we all have an equal say. There are too many of us. It is not feasible. There must be a group of men and women, altruists, who work for the common good."

"And so the structure that will be set in place, whereby they incur no expenses in anything, yet nor can they increase their holdings, is designed to accommodate the natural human instinct for greed?"

"Again, exactly. By taking away the impulse for self, we are enabling those men and women the freedom to care only about the good of all. The design is so simple. Listen, Gerardo, when you play any sweepstakes for any company, there is always a disclaimer: no employee is eligible to play. Neither can their family members. If they do, they are fired. We take it a step further. We provide them a comfortable life, not opulent, not Spartan, but comfortable. We then monitor the financial, and only the financial, activities of their family and friends. Should there be a breech in the arrangement, the police end it."

"But how does that system allow people the freedom to choose their lives, to learn how to better themselves? Does not constant surveillance inhibit those people and their aspirations?"

"Yes. It does. But, we have the benefit of technology. We can simply encode the family and friends. They do not know they are being monitored and those who are scanning the information do not know about whom they are reading. Essentially, what is sought is not a particular person or action, but rather a pattern of activity. One or two actions can be tolerated, even excused. But a pattern of activity indicates a person looking out for himself in the short term. It shows a lack of long term vision. That is unacceptable. We need people who can see that together we are strong. We need men who see a future twenty years from now that is better; men who know that that future begins today. We will succeed because we are taking the lessons of revolution and learning. We have learned. We must separate ourselves and give our people a system in which to flourish for who they are, and we will revolutionize the world."

What struck Gerardo then for the first time was the realization that he was the future for his country. His uncle, great man though he was, was old. Gerardo felt his heart stop as he realized why he was called by his uncle to come to Santiago.

===

Chapter Thirteen: Dr. Ogilvie
Office of the Dean, School of Business

JT arrived early wearing a button down shirt with a sport coat. He would have worn a tie, but they all had stains. He had even ironed his pants. With the time overnight to think, the possibilities of study abroad became apparent. This was an opportunity he did not want to miss. Despite everything in his life, he knew he had to live his life. For some reason, opportunities were coming his way. Quick decisions were something that would come to define his life. This was his first. JT woke that morning and felt great. It was a good decision. With the few minutes of wait time, JT hoped to get a peek at the doctor who would be questioning him.

Dr. Ogilvie, meanwhile, had just finished speaking with the Dean and was peering out through a crack in the office door at JT. The kid looked sharp, calm and prepared. Good signs. Then, a thin smile crept across his lips; JT was not reading the magazine in his hand. In fact, his eyes, while seemingly focused on the page, were actually scanning the periphery. The doctor was impressed. This kid was batting a thousand. Was there a homerun in there?

As he opened the door, he noticed the quick look of startle on JT's face. JT, for his part, was a little surprised to see a man, who he supposed was the doctor, walking out of the office. Was the Dean being questioned? JT scanned him up and down: middle age, wiry gray hair, bad teeth (probably coffee, or cigarettes, or both), and nice little pot belly. Yep, this guy was a doctor, alright.

"JT is it? I'm Dr. Ogilvie. Nice to meet you."

"Hi. Nice to meet you, too."

They stepped inside the office, and Dean Bulgiuno excused himself. Now alone, JT could feel eyes on his every move. But every time he glanced at the doctor, he did not even seem to be noticing JT.

"Can I get you a cup o' joe, JT? Or tea? Cream and sugar?"

"A cup of coffee would be great, sir. And, um, one cream, two sugars, please."

Dr. Ogilvie handed the cup over.

"Now listen JT, before we get started, let's run down why we are both here today. I just need to go over the generalities of travel, some of the pitfalls, for people who have had, well, serious emotional events in their recent past. So long as you are open and honest with me, I am quite certain you will get the green light from the school. So, any questions?"

"Just one, sir. Who are you?"

"Good question. Well, my name is Dr. Christopher Ogilvie. I am a practicing psychiatrist with a private practice. I do some side work for universities, which is why I am here today, as well as some small firms. I grew up in Chicago, but moved to the East Coast for college. The University of Pennsylvania had the misfortune of accepting me as an undergrad, and they passed the buck to Harvard for med school. My mother still lives in Chicago, but my sister lives in Miami. Between you and me, I think the wind got to her."

JT liked this guy. He was a little goofy, but his background certainly sounded impressive. As he sipped his coffee and listened to the bio, he felt himself sliding deeper into the chair.

As the kid crossed his legs and took a sip, Dr. Ogilvie made a mental note. He was relaxing. A few anecdotes from college, including an embarrassing night out, and the young man even smiled. Then, quietly, Dr. Ogilvie made a reference to his own father's passing.

"It happened so fast, the paramedics said he was dead on contact. The car did not even slow down. As he blew through that stop sign and hit my father's car, witnesses said it seemed like he hit the gas harder to keep his speed. I was away at college, at UPenn. I took the rest of the semester off to stay at home. My sister went back to Miami; she was older, newly married. It was just me and my mom.

When I returned to school, it took some doing, but with the help of friends, and the school, I was able to have a successful college career. And so here I am today."

===

Chapter Fourteen: ¡*Bienvenidos*!
Santiago, Chile

JT stepped off the plane and half-mumbled, half-cursed. He had boarded the plane from New York in shorts and a t-shirt. New York's thermometers read 79 degrees. As he stepped off the plane he remembered what he wanted to remember when he was packing his carry-on bag: Chile is in South America and South America has seasons which are opposite to North America. So, 79 degrees in New York meant it was cold in Santiago. Freezing, as it turned out. JT grabbed the light windbreaker he had and wrapped it around him.

He was in Chile. What the hell was he doing in Chile? Maybe it was the cold that jolted his senses; maybe it was the thirteen hour flight in a cramped coach seat. Whatever it was, JT needed to sit down. He needed to wrap his head around the very real fact that his life was literally upside-down.

When he had gone into Dean Bulgiuno's office with his decision made, he did so with the desire to study in Europe. That was partly how he convinced himself to commit. This was a chance to travel which the school was throwing at him, why not Europe? He had studied Italian and Greek, and with his Spanish growing, he felt confident he could travel the entire continent. With most Americans unable to speak two languages, he knew even an attempt in another language would win him points with the multi-lingual Europeans.

The Dean had different ideas, however. According to him, Dr. Ogilvie recommended South

ng point for JT. Due to the history
IS, most Europeans had
s of Americans. They were not all
nced travelers they meant nothing.
..... who was perhaps a little
.......able, Europe could prove difficult and
frustrating. South America, on the other hand, was
still opening itself to tourists and visitors. After years
in which various countries had various dictatorships,
terrorist groups and revolutions, the continent as a
whole was settling. Of course there were still
problems socially, economically and politically –
countries don't change their stripes overnight!
Nonetheless, the average South American man or
woman was open to meeting new people, especially
Americans. Chile, with its strong and growing
economy, would give JT new possibilities he had not
thought of before precisely because he had always
looked to Europe when he was learning languages.
The people were friendly, and the culture was rich in
its heritage of music, dance, and literature. In Chile,
JT could more fully develop his Spanish. At the same
time, Santiago was a cosmopolitan city, so he could
also find some Italian speakers with whom to practice.

"Listen, JT," said the Dean, "we want you to
study abroad, we want you to have time. But we don't
want to throw you to the dogs. Dr. Ogilvie, in looking
at the possibilities, feels this might work best for
several reasons. Some of them I've named, but there
are a few others which might seem odd. The first is
the climate. Santiago is relatively similar to the
Philadelphia-DC climate. And even though it is
reversed because it is on the other side of the equator,

the fluctuations, once you acclimatize yourself to the immediate reversal, will feel natural. Secondly, the history is akin to US history, just with a Spanish flavor. Not to oversimplify it, but they were colonized by a European power, the Indians were excluded, and the people fought a revolution to gain their independence. That understanding of a foreign ruling nation, of forefathers who fought for the dream of a new nation, will place you on a balance with some of the locals. Chileans, for the most part, are very welcoming of Americans. As a student, your language skills and studies will be appreciated and, from past experience, we know that most of our study abroad students make friends quickly and easily in Chile."

There was some more cajoling and discussion. JT was a little discombobulated because he had not even thought of Chile. Nevertheless, the Dean was making good points, ones which did not even occur to him.

"JT, you want to go to Europe. That's your first choice. Study abroad is meant to be a chance to explore new territory, to go where you would not. But think about it; you were focused on Europe. And given your druthers, you would go there. You would not go to Chile. You would not go to South America. Europe will be there next year, and you will go there to see Spain, Italy and Portugal. But, should you turn this down, you probably will not return to South America. Take this chance. Do what so few have the courage to do when they study."

"Well, what about Greece, Dean? I was not only hoping for Western Europe, but I was also hoping to travel and visit some of Eastern Europe, go to some classical archaeological sites, museums and galleries. I won't be able to do any of that from South America."

"We took that into account. We know what you were hoping for this coming year. In discussions with Dr. Ogilvie, we agreed that completely changing your wishes was not beneficial for you, either. It's one thing to convince you to push your limits, it's another to force you to change. Therefore, we explored the programs in that area and we think we have one that would allow you to visit the region and still work on classes which will count towards a degree. Interested?"

JT sat there with a big goofy grin on his face. The Dean had to hide his. This kid was going to go to Chile. And he was probably going to Egypt.

"The program is at the American University in Cairo. The school is an English speaking school. You will have four classes. Fortunately for foreign non-Muslim students, this coming Spring is full of Eids, or Muslim holidays. As a result, you will have close to five weeks free time from school. That should give you enough time to travel the region, visit neighboring countries like Greece, or even Malta. Do just about whatever can jump into that head of yours. You see, JT, we are looking for a balance between what you want and what the doctor thinks is most beneficial for you. This could be the best year of your life. All you have to do is say, 'Yes'."

And he did. He wanted to get out and travel and live and see what the world had to offer. Well, this was the first offer, and he took it. When he returned to his room, he sat down to come to grips with his decision. He had just decided not only to actually study overseas, but he agreed to study in two places which had only ever crossed his mind in geography class: Chile and Egypt. Chile was the more pressing concern since he would be traveling there first. JT stood up and walked over to see Janey. He was going to be reading quite a bit on this country, and he wanted Janey to be reading the same things. He wanted her to know what he would know. He hoped this would help her understand. He hoped it would help him understand.

In their reading, JT was impressed with the history of Chile. Sure, like most of the Americas, the Europeans massacred the Indians and the Indians fought bravely, but what struck him was the richness of the native area. The native Araucanians seemed to have left their impact on the Spanish settlers. Unconquered by the Incas, or their conquerors the Spaniards, the Chilean Indians had a fierce and poetic spirit. It seemed as if the land emitted some mystical element of beauty and splendor and passion. The Araucanians had it, and the Chilean *mestizos* of today demonstrate it. Their revolutions and rebellions over the past few centuries were not simply grabs for power or prestige, but a move for greater independence of the Chilean spirit. Even the Pinochet dictatorship in the late twentieth century, as misguided and brutal as it was, evidenced strains of that idea. And the Chilean spirit corrected itself in 1988, voting out the dictatorship. The poetry of Mistral, Neruda, and Parra brought JT crashing into the Chilean mind. The folk style of Victor Jara jolted JT's senses. The passion and the resolve of the people with whom he was about to spend half a year heartened JT, and even Janey felt that JT might see some good from this experience.

All of this ran through his mind sitting in Santiago, Chile. Here in the airport, waiting to be picked up by the bus sent by the Program of Studies, he was noting the difference in the environment in the airport. In such a seemingly innocuous environment, there were several that stuck him. The first was the number of armed guards, *heavily* armed guards. They were not simply wearing side-arms, but had rifles and automatics slung over their shoulders. The second difference JT assumed was, at least partially, related to this: the people were comfortable and relaxed. No one seemed worried about their bags or their children. No one seemed in a rush, and no one tried to push ahead of anyone else. People were pleasantly speaking to one another and genuinely enjoying their time in the airport.

Yup, thought JT, it might be similar, but it is definitely different.

===

Chapter Fifteen: Los Cotarín
Santiago, Chile

    The first couple days in Santiago were not so bad.
The Program of Studies had provided several field
trips around the city and given some foot tours so the
students did not feel so vulnerable. In the process, JT
had met some good people and started to form
friendships. It was an interesting bunch of students
who decided to go to Chile. But what most struck him
was the certitude with which they had chosen Chile.
Whereas he had known little to nothing, they each
seemed to him as being well versed in several areas of
Chilean life, either politics and poetry, or history and
religion, or sports. Thus, his trips around the city not
only afforded him a chance to learn his new environs,
but also learn something about each of his classmates.
    What he was unsure of was the family with
whom he would be living. Neither the Dean nor the
program offered much information. The only
information was their names and the length of time for
which they had housed foreign students. JT's family
was the Cotarín family: a mother, a father, and two
brothers. JT was twenty years old, and the brothers
were eighteen and twenty-two. Beyond that
information, JT knew little. So, the day of
introduction, JT was a little nervous. With this family
he would be living, eating, sleeping, and speaking.
But he was as ready as he was going to be.
    Introductions were a mess. Each family was
supposed to arrive at a certain time, but, with the hotel

in the middle of downtown, arrivals and departures
were not so crisp. In the confusion JT found the
family after a ten minute search. To greet him were
the mother and the father. They shook his hand,
kissed his cheek and beamed with joy to meet him. JT
felt instantly at ease. The only awkward moment was
when the father would not let him carry his own bag.
It was awkward because JT felt weird letting someone
else carry his bags when he was capable, and it was
awkward because in his nervousness, JT's Spanish
sounded like a child's.

"Um, *yo poder llevar las maletas de yo.*"

"*No, m'ijo, está bien, te las llevo. Cálmate.
¡Bienvenidos a Chile!*"

JT's Spanish could only improve from that,
and as his face retreated from red to pink to his natural
hue, the car ride provided him a glimpse of downtown
Santiago. Carlo was the father, nice and friendly, but
clearly very set and disciplined in his mannerisms. He
was average height, balding and with a moustache
bushy, but neatly trimmed. The mother was Berta.
She was a little shorter, but made a strong first
impression. She was quiet in the car, but when she
spoke to Carlo, he reacted. JT wondered what
impression he made on them as he alternately
scrambled to follow the conversation and get his
bearings on his surroundings.

The car pulled up to the house with the
brothers waiting outside. Ignacio was older, about
JT's height and a little stockier, with a full face and a
jovial expression. Pato was taller and thinner, with a
deeper expression about him. Whereas Ignacio had
more of a coiffed hairstyle, Pato had his hair high and

tight, though both were neatly trimmed.

The next few weeks JT and the family came to know one another, and a routine was in place. The hardest part for JT was adjusting his internal schedule for a 9 p.m. dinner. He had eaten at 5:30 – 6 at night for most of his life, and the first few weeks with the Cotarín's his stomach was making noises noticeable from the other room. But, like most things, JT adjusted. After a few weeks, he even started to spend time with the brothers and their groups of friends. He met cute girls, had interesting talks with the guys about politics and their relations with the US, and learned that his new favorite *fútbol* team in Chile was supposed to be La U – La Universidad de Chile.

It was not until a month into his stay that JT learned that all the men worked for the Chilean government, more specifically, the military. That explained the well trimmed hair on all of them. The father was a bureaucrat working in the Ministry of Defense. Ignacio was doing some kind of double duty with finance and engineering, probably with the aerospace sector. Pato was in flight school, working to become a fighter pilot.

==

"So what do they do?" asked Janey.

"Well, it's kind of weird. They are all in the military or defense, somehow. It's like I was placed with a family of Pattons."

"Do they act military? I mean, are they strict, waking up at dawn, that kind of stuff?"

"No, they seem normal enough. It appears to be just a job for them. They talk about it a bit, but nothing too in depth."

"What are you going to do? Anything?"

Good question, thought JT. Was there anything he could? Was there anything *to* do?

"I don't know. I like hearing some of the stories and they seem to like to tell stories of their history and heroes. It's neat. I never heard of this stuff before, but there are so many fascinating events that occurred here."

"Tell me one, and then maybe I'll let you off the phone."

"Okay, but you have to promise to write me a letter as soon as we hang up. Anyway, there was this admiral named Arturo Pratt..."

==

"So what do we do?"

"Nothing. We keep going as if all is well and good."

"And then?"

"And then, they contact us. Then we act. Not until then. *¿Cachai?*"

"*Sípo.*"

===

Chapter Sixteen: An Internship
Santiago, Chile

A month and a half into his stay, Ignacio offered to take JT to the mall. It was a lazy Saturday, overcast but bright, and cold enough for a windbreaker or sweater. On the ride over, JT tried to figure out what it was about Chile that felt so comfortable for him. The cars and buildings were similar to home. The clothing style was similar, if more casual and folksy, but that did not necessarily make a difference. The people were friendly and approachable, but he always felt that home was like that, too. The language did not even strike him as a hindrance or obstacle to that comfort level. He glanced at Ignacio driving and talking and tried to see it in his face. Many characteristics of the Chilean people were in his face, and all of them impressed JT. But none of them was what made him feel so comfortable.

They continued driving and pulled in to the mall parking lot, chatting and laughing as Ignacio schooled JT in music trends and soap operas.

"Guys down here really involve themselves with soap operas?" asked JT.

"Absolutely," said Ignacio, "the characters are big stars. They make appearances and promote products and many, many men want to try out for the next soap opera. What is so strange for you about this?"

"It's just that back home, only girls watch soap operas. The stereotype is a housewife, or older woman, watching the soaps all day and then gabbing on the phone with a friend. Guys tend to mock that and go watch sports at a bar."

"But do you not see the similarities? The athletes you watch grab your attention because they live the life you dream, they drive the car you want. It is the same for soap operas. Many men watch here because they want to be smooth when they speak with women, just like the men on TV. But, eh, maybe American men do not have the confidence" finished Ignacio, indicating down with his finger and bursting into laughter.

The two kept chatting and joking as they walked through the mall. Ignacio showed JT the music stores, the clothing stores and, what was most important, the soccer store. JT bought a windbreaker and a jersey.

"Shall we celebrate your acceptance of La U as the best soccer team over a cup of coffee?" offered Ignacio.

==

As they found a table and sat down, Ignacio asked JT to tell him about home. He had never been to the United States, and while he was hoping to get there one, that day may be preceded by others.

"Sure," said JT. "What do you want to know?"

"*Todo. Dime todo*" was the answer.

"But I thought you knew a lot about the US? What do you want me to say?"

"Yes, I do know a lot, but only because I read. It is not because I have been there, or experienced life there. I want to hear what it is like from the mouth of someone who has."

"That's kind of broad, so I'll just start with my home town and go from there. So, where to begin? I am from Philadelphia, the northeast part of the city."

And so JT regaled Ignacio with stories of his childhood, of growing up in a big family and of sharing a bedroom. He even made a station wagon seem like a good idea.

All the while, Ignacio was watching JT, noticing how excited he was to be discussing Philadelphia and his life.

"JT, you have good memories of Philadelphia, yes?"

"Yes, of course. Why?"

"And you are having a wonderful time in Chile, yes?"

"Yes, so far I love everything about it."

"Well, I have an idea that might just suit you. I have a colleague who sits on the board of an international trade group, the Santiago and Philadelphia Chamber of Commerce of Pennsylvania. Your hometown, no? Anyway, they need someone to act as a liaison, someone who would be willing to travel back and forth from Santiago to Philadelphia. The work is mostly analytical, with some socializing. They present you with the research they have gathered. You would have to look at it and discuss the merits or faults with various member organizations in both countries. Would you be interested?"

"I don't know, Ignacio. I mean, I'm only in college. Don't get me wrong, I love the idea of it, traveling back and forth. But, this level of work responsibility may be over my head."

"No, no. Don't think so much. My colleague tells me it is quite easy. The main problem with filling the position is not the work, but the role. So many people do not want to travel. But you have a connection to both places. You are young, so you are more mobile. And, if you do this now, when you do finish college, you will have contacts in business from all over the world. How is this bad for you?"

Hard to argue that, thought JT. And, if he could travel back and forth he would. Chile was breathtaking in its scenery, the nightlife and the culture had engaged him fully and their outdoor sports were world class. As he sipped his coffee, he thought back to the meeting in the office with the dean:

"Do what so few have the courage to do." Was this one of those opportunities? Was this a chance to see what he had?

"If I was to do this, how would I even start?"

"The biggest problem would be introducing you to him. He is very busy, and very important, and so does not take the time to meet new people without reason. So, I had an idea. You play rugby, yes? Well, so does he. He and I are in the same club in the city. It is casual, but the competition is strong. How good are you?"

JT smiled. He had joined rugby as a sophomore because he had started to gain weight after baseball season. He wanted a reason to exercise in the fall and winter months. He picked it up quickly, though, and by the end of sophomore year he was starting on the A side.

"I can play."

"Good, then we will go sometime in the next couple of weekends. I will arrange it for you to be on his team. Watch him, run with him, help him and work with him. But do not try to say anything out of the ordinary to him. In other words, only talk about rugby. This colleague, Gerardo, is very quick and he will notice if you ask him about business after just having met him. We will wait. After the game, we will casually talk to him about the game. We will steer the conversation and mention that you are from the States and, more specifically, from Philadelphia. Mention that you like Chile, and hope to be able to return for a visit after you return home. He will pick up the cue from there. Any questions?"

Sipping his coffee, JT scanned Ignacio. He pondered a moment and then, "Yes, in fact, I do have some. How do you say 'ruck-over' and 'scrum' in Spanish?"
==

The next two weeks, Ignacio and JT practiced some to wipe the rust off, and Ignacio gave vocabulary lessons for rugby in Spanish.

The day of the game was almost too perfect. JT had been mainly a scrum-half, but had played fly-half also. Gerardo was the team's scrum. Fortunately, the regular fly was injured just enough that he wanted to sit out this game, so JT was able to step right in his slot. The game went well, and several times the play between JT and Gerardo was what advanced their team.

JT was glad the traditional drink-up was not limited as an American college thing. He always enjoyed talking to the other team and laughing about the game afterwards. Today, though, he was much more careful with his beer intake than a normal drink-up. He grabbed a beer and walked over to Gerardo, knowing Ignacio was watching.

"Hey, Gerardo, I just want to say nice game. I normally play scrum, but watching you I realized there are still some things for me to learn. My name's JT."

Gerardo took his hand and thanked him.

"What is that accent? American?"

"Hey, Gerardo, how are you?" chimed in Ignacio as he walked over just then. "I see you've met JT. He's living with us this semester. Pretty good player, no?"

The three of them chit-chatted for a few minutes about the game and rugby. And then, to the surprise of JT and Ignacio, Gerardo turned the conversation to JT's home.

"So you are from the States? What part? The accent sounds northeastern."

"I'm from Philadelphia, and I am attending university in Washington, DC."

"I take it you've been to Chile before and that is why you came to study."

"Actually, no. I had not even read a full paragraph on Chile, let alone visit, before I came here. My school dean suggested it. While at first I was a little unsure of the wisdom of my agreement, I can tell you now that I can't imagine not having Chile in my brain. This is a remarkable country."

Genuinely caught up in the moment, JT turned to Ignacio and continued to gush about Chile, the scenery, the outdoors, the literature he had read – any and everything which took his breath away. Meanwhile, Gerardo was watching JT, impressed by the energy he showed in discussing that which was important to him. And Gerardo knew the accent, he knew this kid from the northeast was either blueblood or blue collar. His enthusiasm and innocence in description betrayed it, blue collar. Foreign travel was a genuinely new experience for him. He was enjoying it, too. Good for him, thought Gerardo. And he thought. Having just played with him and having seen the athleticism, he was struck with the possibilities this new college student presented.

"JT, what are you studying here in Chile?" asked Gerardo.

"Well, I'm splitting my classes. I have two business courses at the Catholic University, and two liberal arts classes at La U."

"Listen, JT, if you are interested in business and maybe gaining some actual international experience, I may have something for you. How's that sound?"

"Wow, that would be great. That would truly impress my dean."

Impress the dean, just incredible; Gerardo was very happy he had played rugby today.

"Good, then I'll call Ignacio here next week and we'll set something up. Again, nice meeting you. Ciao."

The three exchanged handshakes.

Ignacio smiled at JT.

"I think we just found you an internship."

===

Chapter Seventeen: Agent Chris Grelsh

Chris Grelsh spent most of his youth scraping by. Before he was seven years old, his parents died while vacationing on a cruise. He never learned the details of the tragedy; he knew only that they had drowned. The next six years he was in and out of foster homes. Then, just as he was entering high school, he found a decent home in which he could be a contributing member. The father married late, having enjoyed the bachelor's life until he was 40. The mother had done the same, except until she was 48. When they met, they knew they wanted children, but she was not prepared for pregnancy. So they become foster parents. Problem was, they both still enjoyed the nightlife and were barely home. They often spent entire weekends away from the house.

Chris knew that it was not the quintessential family model, but in its own way it was solid and stable. He had a roof over his head, and, being alone so often, he had to take care of things around the house. When he had been there a year, he knew that there was a chance for better things. He knew that "better" anything was not always immediate, but as he passed day 365, he knew better was worth waiting for in his life.

In school, he never had that one teacher who became a mentor or role model. Instead, he had a string of solid, concerned and dedicated teachers who made small efforts to show how there was good and beauty in life if the mind was open. Combined with the home life he had, Chris hooked into his chance, buckled down and worked. He worked hard in school and he worked hard at his after school jobs. Finishing high school, he was not at the top of the class, but he was voted Salutatorian almost unanimously. His dedication, diligence, and calm demeanor won over the school in his time there.

At first, college was not what Chris wanted. He was good with his hands, and he was a quick learner when it came to analyzing situations. His part-time job as an auto mechanic seemed perfect. He had to assess the problem and fix it. So he decided against college and went to work full-time.

Things were fine for two years, but he was going nowhere. The owner's promises of night school and apprenticeship never materialized. As a matter of fact, Chris' tasks were increasing, but not as a mechanic. The boss wanted him to start getting the coffee and the office lottery tickets. Chris felt trapped and confused. He had let school pass him and now was seeing his trade pass him, too. Barely twenty years old, he felt washed up.

One morning, frustrated and tired, Chris bought his first lottery ticket, his own lottery ticket. The jackpot was $10 million. When he walked back to the garage, he was smiling. He was thinking about what he could do should he win. He was so excited by the end of the day he rushed home to watch the winning numbers on TV. He was so sure he'd win that he already had a gift list running in his head. He didn't. But it sparked the idea he had kept dormant since school: there is hope if you are open to it. Even in losing he had more passion in those few moments than he had in two years. Something was missing, and the reality of the lottery, so simple, struck him hard and fast: if you only wait for others to help, you wait. He dove into his work and started doing odd jobs on weekends. He moved the TV to the closet and signed up for a library card. Eventually, even his boss could not ignore the excellent work he was doing, and started to increase his responsibility.

Chris kept playing the lottery once a month, mostly to let his mind wander about what to do with the winnings. He loved to sit back after work with a beer and a cigar and watch the sun set as he dreamed that he was watching it from his own yacht. As time passed, he saw changes. With more responsibility and odd jobs, with no cable bill and no internet bill, he saw more money in his pocket. That helped with the material things, as his bank account slowly increased. He bought a nicer car, nicer clothes. With his extra free time, he was re-learning his high school Spanish and Latin American history. And those nights of dreaming of his own yacht helped him to remain focused. He knew the changes he was making could lead to his own yacht. The lottery ticket would not get him what he wanted, he had to work for it. So he went back and applied to college. He walked to a military recruiting office, just to see what possibilities lay before him. He was accepted into a program at St. Joseph's University in Philadelphia. Chris needed to take three night classes before beginning in order to bring him back up to speed, and he could then enroll full time, under the mentorship of a professor. He would be a college freshman at the ripe age of 23. No matter, he thought, at least it's my life that I am making.

Everything was going according to plan, and

Chris never felt better. He found an apartment and moved out. His weekends alone were now his choice. He actually spent more time with his foster parents by having dinner during the week at the house. Even though he barely had time to sleep eight hours, he felt refreshed every morning he woke up. He thought his life was moving up and could not get better.

Then he won. He hit for $213 million.

After taxes and depreciation, he took home $110 million dollars. The first few weeks, he was stunned. He had the sense to wait a few months before collecting his winnings and also not to hold a press conference. He just drove in to the lottery office, had the money transferred to his account, and went home. Hesitant at first, his first attempt of enjoying the money was not clipping coupons. It felt good not worrying about the price of groceries. Next, he want to Macy's and did the same; bought himself a suit. Finally, he went to a tailor, and had a suit custom made. It fit extremely well. And it felt incredible not worrying about the $890 price tag.

He did not tell anyone what happened to him. But, his foster parents were starting to become suspicious that he was dressing so sharply. He told them he hit for a couple hundred thousand, and paid for a trip to Tahiti. They stopped asking questions.

Treating himself, taking care of his family, and enjoying his increasing financial independence all were wonderful, but quitting his job may have been the best feeling of all. His boss was speechless and begged him to stay. He offered to increase his pay, his days off, anything and everything to convince him to stay. Chris thanked him for his kindness, and walked out. The whole scene reinforced for him the importance of doing your work well. His boss did not want him to stay because of anything that had to do with money; he wanted him to stay because he had become a stellar and consistent contributor to the company. His absence would be felt by employees and customers, alike. He went to the night classes and earned straight A's. He came onto campus at St. Joe's and tried to blend in to the crowds. Being older, he did not fall into the underclass nightlife, but instead fell into classes. After a year, he decided he wanted to work in international relations. He transferred to the program and added second, third and fourth languages to his linguistic skills. With that in mind, he joined ROTC. He wanted to get a peek into training and opportunities after school.

In his senior year, his story made its way up the ROTC chain of command. It was certainly unique. A recruiter who had special orders to notice such cases forwarded his name to the NSA. They watched him for months and studied his studies. The agents were amazed. Chris had added not only languages, but also European and Middle Eastern history to his reading. The library database with his history of books borrowed was the biggest they had ever seen. They checked and double-checked all their records because no one could believe this guy was for real, or that he had come so far so quietly.

He was approached in the beginning of his second semester of senior year. He was 27.

He took it.

What sold Chris was the possibility to make a difference using his knowledge. He successfully passed through the evaluations and training, and he was to join a secret operation about whose existence even the President was barely aware. The program was similar to government programs searching the skies for alien life in its structure and financing, but was not officially included in any documents or even publicly discussed. The name alone was known only to about ten people who were not directly involved.

The program's name was "MacNessa", and it required all of Chris' energy, skill and focus. At the beginning, it provided Chris a motivation to keep learning, working and hoping for the best. Over time, the importance of it took over his life and guided his every move, his every thought, his every action. This program helped Chris recruit and secure low-level, though functional, agents. JT was one of these agents.
==

When Chris received the phone call from the Dean, he was expecting another solid review for a candidate, but nothing out of the ordinary. It was this kid's hobbies which piqued his interest: this was a student willing to go to a foreign country, to a language he did not speak, just to be close to the possibility of getting to Greece to work with his interest in ancient Greek. This was a recruit with whom he could work.

He set up the interview and donned his interview persona, Dr. Ogilvie. The story line changed as he needed it, and reviewing this kid's file, he knew instantly what he needed to say to snare him. For his cover, the artists at NSA were incredible. His pot belly and poor teeth looked so real he thought about changing his diet on the car ride over to the Dean's office. Scanning the office, he configured the set-up so he knew where JT would be sitting. It was in the line of sight of the office door.

During the interview, JT continued to impress with his knowledge, his willingness to experience new things, and, unbeknownst to him, his openness to suggestion. It would take some maneuvering, and a gentle touch, but he knew he could bring him on board if it would give JT a sense of pleasing an adult male figure, someone he could trust, someone who understood him. Someone like Dr. Ogilvie.

==

Chris was devastated when he heard JT was taken. Crushed. Over time, he had grown genuinely fond of him. Maybe it was the circumstances, or something of himself he saw in JT. Whatever it was, Chris felt an indisputable paternal instinct with him. Actually looked to him as a son-figure, if that even existed.

When the package came from Janey, he recognized the name instantly. As it was addressed to "Dr. Ogilvie", he put aside. He thought it would be another one of her letters pleading for information. For the first year after JT did not return from Chile, he must have received three a month.

"Let it go, Janey" he whispered to himself as he tossed this package on the corner of his desk.

"We have to do that sometimes." Then he loosened his tie, poured himself a whiskey and water, and sat down to watch the sun set.

===

Chapter Eighteen: JT's First Contact
Santiago, Chile

A few days after playing rugby with Gerardo, Ignacio had to go to the south to look into some projects. For a few weeks, JT had not spent that much time with Pato, but now Pato took to inviting him out on the weekends, and meeting up with his friends during the week for coffee.

In the meantime, JT's internship was going well. Gerardo was very kind the first couple of days, working with him to acclimate to the office, his role and his responsibilities. They sat down and looked over both JT's school schedule and what trips he was hoping to take. With that in mind, they planned several trips before his semester was finished. They also looked into living arrangements for the summer after the semester so JT could continue working until he had to return to school full time. And while Gerardo did not guarantee a position beyond that, he hinted that, should JT do well, there was no reason to rule out a continued role.

With all this time together, JT became quite accustomed to Gerardo's schedule and, looking to get in well with him, met him with an "extra" coffee, or asked his advice on a point of work. Gerardo liked this; saw it as a motivated worker looking to impress his boss. It was working.

Every time he went out with Pato, he gushed about how well work was going, and how much he spoke to Gerardo, and how they both were making great plans for the trips back to the States.

"So, JT, your work, *¿es bueno?*" asked Pato.

"*Sí, sí, es bueno.* I like it a lot."

"And Gerardo, what's he like?"

"Well, he's great. I know he has much responsibility and so many people look to him for advice and guidance. Knowing that, and that he still takes the time to work directly with me, makes me feel like a real contributor, you know? I'm not sure where this can go and what possibilities this opens for me but I do know that by working with him, great things will come my way and I will have the opportunity to make a real difference."

Yes, you will, thought Pato. Yes, you will.

==

After a month, Pato dropped 150 pesos into the phone.

"Hello?"

"*Buenos días.* He is ready. Talk to him. Tomorrow, his class ends at noon, and before work he stops at the coffee shop around the corner from his office."

"*Gracias.* We'll make sure to get his attention."

"Good luck. *Ciao.*"

"*Adiós.*"

==

"*Buenos días, señor gringo. ¿Cómo está Ud. hoy día?* "

"*Hola*, Mariela. I'm well. How are you today?"

"*Super-bien, gracias.* You want the normal, *¿sí ?*"

"*Sí*, one coffee with milk, and *un café negro.*"

JT dropped his pesos on the counter as Mariela whipped around to get his coffees. He had a nice little routine going here. Mariela had been really nice the first few times he came into the shop and fumbled around with the order. After that, he felt comfortable enough to ask which bus to take somewhere, or how much he should pay in a cab for a certain ride. Soon, if he had a few minutes and the café was slow, he would hang out and chat with her. She was easy to talk to about nothing, and it was even fun chastising her for calling him "señor" – she was at least two years his senior. After classes and before work, this was a great way to rejuvenate and find a smile.

"Here is your coffee, señor."

"*Gracias*, Mariela. Can I buy you a cup of coffee?"

Mariela smiled and her eyes visibly twinkled. She liked this gringo, he was fun.

"Maybe another day, *señor*. Right now, there is a man in the corner who keeps staring at you. I imagine he is waiting to have a coffee with you."

JT turned around and sure enough, there was a man looking straight at him. When they made eye contact, he pushed out a chair.

Turning around, JT saw Mariela shrug; she had no idea who he was.

JT thanked her and walked over to the man, confused but curious about some stranger staring at him.

"Can I help you?" JT offered.

"No, but I can help you... if you have a moment?"

==

Twenty minutes later, JT called the office and let them know he was unexpectedly running late – he would not be in for another 40 minutes.

"I don't believe you. I don't even know who the hell you are. Why should I believe a word you say? Why should I even believe your name is José Luis?"

"All fair questions. All fair."

José Luis sipped his coffee as he pondered this challenge. This young man was exactly as he had been described.

"Let's start with this: Do you believe I work for the US Government?"

"Okay, yeah, I'll buy that. You have too much work here to be making this up just for a laugh."

"Good. Do you believe that some of the documents and photos I showed you are real and unaltered? At least *some* of them?"

Damn, some of them had to be real.

"Again, okay, I'll buy that some of them are real. So?"

"Well, then, think about it. If even a couple of these documents and photos are real, the implications are mind-boggling and, in the extreme, dangerous to all of us, every man, woman and child. Does this mean nothing to you?

Let's look at your host family, shall we? As I am certain you know by now, every one of them is connected to the military or the police. And they are doing well: they live in the best neighborhood, attended the best schools, date the prettiest girls. We have been tracking them and while we have no concrete proof, it is probable that they might know what is happening, what the plans are for Chile. And you are living in their house! Does this escape you? Does this connection between your host family and the information I've provided you simply skirt past your eyes?"

"Honestly, I don't know. Do I want people to get hurt or die? No, of course not. But do I care, as in, do I think this will affect my life? Right now, no. Besides, what does this have to do with me?"

"We have been working on this for years, busting our asses to work both effectively and covertly. Because we can't make this public, we have been limited in our capabilities. But you, in less than one-half a year, have saddled up to the prime suspect in all of Latin America and have access not even dreamed about by anyone in the office or in the field. All you would have to do is stay close to Gerardo. Keep getting him coffee, and keep playing rugby with him. Be smooth, but persistent and gain his trust. Even little info like appointment schedules will help immensely and may help save us all.

As far as what this has to do with you, let me let you in on a little secret, he *will* cut you loose the second he does not need you. Look at these files, look at this track record. He is a master of manipulating people and moving ahead. He learned from the best, and he is poised to become the best. If he accomplishes what he sets out to do here, you will be nothing to him. Best case scenario for you? You can live, but are arrested and imprisoned for the rest of your life. Worst case, you are *put to death* for knowing too much."

José Luis leaned back to watch JT's reaction. This was a delicate dance. This kid had done nothing to deserve any of this, and dumping it all too fast may push him away. Not giving enough information would make the decision not to help easy. The worst part was that, in the reverse situation, José Luis knew that he himself would not help. This job opportunity for JT was the best thing in his life, and the stories he was hearing were far from normal, far from any reality he had even heard before in his life. It was all, in every sense of the word, fantastic. José Luis looked at this young man, pondering the situation, trying to wrap his head around it all, and wondered if he was doing the right thing.

"Think about this, JT, your country needs you, and you have no parents who will worry about you."

That stung. Both knew it.

"Listen, I appreciate all you must have gone through to find me and compile all this info, but it's not for me. I have a good upswing in my life right now, and when I get home, I plan on getting a good job, and getting married. I am not going to mess that up for some crazy Boogie-man conspiracy story."

José Luis felt the envelope in his pocket and decided to end it.

"Well, JT, I'm done. I will not try to manipulate you into this. This decision must be yours. Best of luck."

Damn, thought José Luis, as he walked out, I actually meant that!

He's leaving? That's it? JT was a little perplexed. What did he mean he would not try to manipulate him? What else did he have to offer? Or threaten?

"Hey, José Luis" shouted JT as he chased after him.

"Yes?"

"What else do I need to know? What are you not telling me?"

"It has nothing to do with words" and he handed over the envelope.

==

Back when "Dr. Ogilvie" had approved of JT, everything and everyone connected to him was monitored. Weakness and opportunities were sought. As a result of his life, however, there were few chances to influence events or situations. Everything JT had stated to José Luis was true, and had nothing interfered, there was every chance it would happen exactly that way. But Grelsh knew they needed this kid, and made clear to everyone an opportunity would arise if they were vigilant; and they damn well better be vigilant. He was correct.

JT had been busy the past few weeks, and his frequent calls became less so. Not much, but enough that Janey was upset. She missed him and hearing his voice soothed her. An attractive girl, she had a few male fans who saw this as an opening. The first to make a move was TJ. He had approached her and asked her out for coffee. When she hesitated, he made a lame joke that "JT was the boyfriend, but by switching the letters, TJ could be her friend who's a boy". It was lame, and both knew it, but it made Janey smile and she accepted. Cameras were snapping like crazy and every attempt by TJ to get closer – holding her hand, touching the small of her back – was captured on film by the agents. Coffee ran for a few hours and as he walked her home, TJ mistook her softness as an invitation. At her door, he went in for a kiss. She pushed him away, but not before the shutter snapped several times. They had it. They had the information. They could maneuver as they wished.

==

JT took the envelope and paused. Was this some kind of bad spy movie? Was he really taking an envelope from a spy trying to recruit him? If he was, what was in the envelope? The realization came slowly to him as he unfolded the envelope. Could it be?

JT walked to a nearby bench as he flipped through the pictures of Janey and some guy holding hands, laughing, having coffee and, worst of all, kissing. His eyes were glued to the photos and his breath was frozen in his lungs. She had been his reason, she had been his hope, she had been his future. He was shattered.

"How do I know these are real? How do I know you did not send in some stooge to set her up?" demanded JT.

"You don't. But remember, I tried to walk away without showing these to you. I did not want this to be your deciding factor even though, I know. I know that you have come to a decision."

"I have."

And he sat there quietly for a few minutes. Neither said anything. JT put the pictures away. He asked to see the information from the folder and quietly, thoughtfully, paged through it all. Everything in his life had left him, in one way or another. By chance or by choice, he was alone. Should be choose to work toward a greater goal? Could he commit himself without fear?

José Luis watched JT's eyes and knew what he was thinking: was it worth it? "JT", he said, "each of us has one shot at life. Life is not easy, life is not calm, life is not predictable. But we can make choices. We can decide our own fate if we take control of it. We do not receive many life-changing choices, but when we do, we must recognize them and seize them. This one is yours."

JT never lifted his head. He simply listened. With a faint nod of the head, he said, "I'm in."

"JT, you must get close to Gerardo, as close as you can. Do whatever it takes. Get to know his schedule, his habits, his contacts, what kind of deodorant he uses, everything. We will be here, and we will make sure nothing happens. I can't thank you enough.

"So that's it? There are no codes, no secret handshakes?"

"No, no" chuckled José Luis, "there are no secret handshakes. As far as communication, I'll be in contact to inform you of how we should be notified. As for now, get to work. You're late. And have a good day."

"Thanks, you too. You off to find another dupe?"

"No, I think I'll grab another cup of coffee from that pretty counter girl."

===

Chapter Nineteen: The Embassy Party
Santiago, Chile

JT spent the next few weeks keeping his routine and watching a little more closely his surroundings. Nothing seemed out of the ordinary, everything was business as usual. But he could not get the pictures and files out of his mind, he could not silence the echo of José Luis's words. As a result, he did work to get closer to Gerardo. The only problem was that Gerardo was working full time, and JT was simply a part-time worker. Getting the coffee, talking about rugby and having Gerardo "mentor" him all allowed him extra face time, but he did not feel that Gerardo looked to him as an asset. Even if José Luis was loony and completely off-base, JT knew he would still need Gerardo's good opinion to move ahead. With the schedule as it was, JT felt that he was missing some incredible people with whom he could connect and try to work later. He just did not see an opportunity. Until it was mentioned to him.

JT missed a few days during the week to work on a school project, and when he arrived on Thursday, Gerardo pulled him aside.

"Listen, JT, I forgot to mention to you earlier, but there is a political event going on tomorrow night at the US Embassy. I wanted you to go, to meet people, and especially since you are American, I thought you might enjoy it. However, the list is closed now for security purposes. I am only telling you because I want you to know that I appreciate your work and have not overlooked you. If I had known you would not be in this week, I would have definitely had your name put on the list. But I kept expecting to see you and so let it slip my mind. I'm sorry."

That is it. If I can get in to that party, thought JT, it will show him that I am clever, dedicated, and willing to do what it takes to accomplish a task. The only problem was getting past security, US Embassy security, which meant US Marines stationed all around.

As JT planned for the party, laying out his suit and tie, shaving and even getting a hair cut, his mind raced for a way into the embassy. All the movies he saw were no help. He was not a professional crook, he had no military experience, and he knew that even one marine was enough to stop him, let alone a whole embassy of marines.

Driving over in the cab, he was borderline panicking about getting arrested and ruining everything for him, for José Luis, even for the Cotarín's – who wants to tell people they hosted a foreign student who then created an international police incident?

"Think, idiot" he muttered to himself. "It's a party, a private party, with a guest list. You cannot get in without being on the list. Someone had to call to put you on the list and, wait, that's it!" The idea was brilliant, and JT simply needed to resuscitate his grade school acting skills.
==

"Good evening, sir, and welcome to the US Embassy. May I have your name please?" enquired the embassy greeter.

"Hi. My name is JT Parral."

"Just a moment, please" as she scanned the list.

"I'm sorry, sir, your name is not here."

"Excuse me? My name should definitely be on the list." He then spelled his name while the greeter continued to scan the list.

"I'm sorry, sir, it is not; and without your name here, I cannot permit you to enter."

"I don't understand. I am an intern for Senator Outis of Pennsylvania and I know that he personally phoned my name in for the list. I don't want to cause a problem, but he expects me to speak to some people inside here on his behalf. I have his number. Should I call him?"

At the mention of the name of a US Senator, the woman became visibly shaken, which helped to divert her attention from JT's shaking. The reality of this working raced through JT's mind and he was nearly frantic in his desire to maintain his self-control.

"Really, I was very much looking forward to tonight and I can call his office" offered JT, with a mix of mock earnestness and mock annoyance at "having" to call.

"Just a moment, sir" said the greeter as she hopped up and ran over to her supervisor.

JT stood at the table and waited, trying to look calm and collected; he had a hand in his pocket and was scanning the room slowly. He had been able to spend a couple weeks working for the Senator, and had had to go through several security checks then. With updates in security, JT knew that his name appearing somewhere in some government database anywhere near the senator's was his only chance of success.

The greeter, meanwhile, was alternately indicating with her hand between JT and the clipboard. Her supervisor pulled out a palm pilot of some sort and JT assumed they were checking some sort of government list. He kept scanning trying not to focus on the supervisor's actions.

Not a minute later, she returned.

"Excuse me, Mr. Parral, I apologize for the confusion; there is no need to bother the senator. Of course, you may enter. Have a lovely night, sir."

"Thank you, miss. I appreciate your help. Have a good night."

JT walked past, half-smiled at the supervisor, avoided eye contact with the marine at the door with the sidearm, and proceeded into the main ballroom. There, he exhaled for the first time since entering the embassy. He had pulled it off. Now he needed a drink. He walked over to the bar, ordered a cocktail, and scanned the room. He needed to find Gerardo and go say hello. He was nowhere in sight. If he decided last minute to switch plans, JT felt he would be caught instantly. In his mind, he needed to be speaking to someone or the marine with the sidearm would come in and take him outside.

Just then, a man walked up to the bar and ordered a drink.

"*Hola,*" said the man.

"*Buenas noches,*" replied JT.

"Oh, American?"

"Why, yes. The accent? In two words?"

"*Sí, sí*, in two words. It is easy to tell. My name is Octavio Ramón de Mojica."

"My name is JT, JT Parral. It's a pleasure to meet you. May I ask, are you here for business or pleasure, or both?"

"You may, and I am here for both. These functions always serve well to discuss topics casually and without obligation, and the embassy does know how to throw a party, as you say. I serve on the board of Chile Oil, and it is good, especially with the ecological concerns anymore, to keep my face known to those who need to know it. And you, young man, business or pleasure?"

"Well, it started as just business, but now that I am here, I am thinking I should try to enjoy myself. I am working part time for the Santiago and Philadelphia Chamber of Commerce of Pennsylvania under the tutelage of Gerardo…"

"Ah, you are Gerardo's young assistant about whom I have heard so much. He told me that your name could not be placed on the guest list. Was he trying to trick me?"

"Oh no, Señor Ramón, he was telling the truth."

"Then, how is it that I am speaking to you now, in this place?"

"Well, I know that Gerardo is trying to care for me, and that being resourceful is of great importance to him. As I was not on the original list, I thought using some resourcefulness to attend tonight would make a good impact on Gerardo. Was that a bad assessment?"

"I would say that your good impact will be noticed. It will be noticed, indeed."

Just then, Gerardo entered the room and was making some introductory rounds. Octavio waved him over.

"Well, well, well. JT. I'm surprised to see you here."

"After speaking to you the other day, and you mentioning that there was an opportunity for me to meet some people, I thought I should take advantage of the chance."

Interesting, thought Gerardo, interesting, indeed.

"Okay, then, young man, let's introduce you. I see you have already met Octavio, the old curmudgeon. Take a look over there at my table, by the dais. Do you see those gentlemen? They are the heads of Chile: the head of La Bolsa, the stock market; the head of Chile Copper; the head of transportation; and the heads of the military branches. These are the people I think you should meet. On more than one of your trips back to Philadelphia, you may be handling their paperwork and selling their ideas. Let's at least give them a face."

JT silently gulped. Holy God, he thought, this guy is hugely influential. Suddenly, his career took a second seat in precedence in his mind.

===

Chapter Twenty: The Prince's Calling
Dublin, Ireland

James hung up the phone and leaned back in his chair. So that was it, they were all coming. Every invite was answered. The gravity of the moment sat on his shoulders and kept him in the chair. His eyes glanced up to the portrait over the fireplace, the portrait of Conor MacNessa.

Conor MacNessa lived at the time of Christ, so the portrait was made on legend and lore. Nonetheless, James felt that Conor was in the painting; had felt it all his life. As a result, he convinced himself that he was destined for greatness as a direct descendant.

James stood up and walked over to the bar, poured himself a whiskey, and looked out the window. His father's home, his family home, had somehow remained in the family possession for hundreds of years, through all the turmoil, the religious battles, the famines. Out this window, he scanned the hillsides lolling into the distance, covered in grass so green it made the rainbow jealous. Running off to the east was a little brook which farther down let into a small loch. As he sipped his whiskey and watched a crow take off from a tree, he thought back on his boyhood.

Every night his father would tell him tales of the glory of Ireland, of the fame of the chivalry and gallantry of the Knights of the Red Branch, of the legendary Cuchullain, of the Fenian cycles and of the heroes of rebellion. In the beginning, James took the stories for just that, stories. James the senior, however, was planting the seed, ingraining the stories, the outcomes, the morals in his son's head.

James chuckled as he recalled his fifteenth birthday. He was awakened by a cannon blast from what he thought was a rusted, useless antique cannon on the back walkway. Looking out the window, he saw his father dressed as he had never seen him: wearing the family tartan, the arms for battle as if it were the year 1500, and his hair braided. When their eyes met, James felt his father sink into his soul. Without a word, James nodded, changed and hurried to his father's side.

They walked in silence for over an hour, James close to his father's heels. Finally, they reached the edge of their property in the far northwest corner. Beyond this cliff point was the ocean. James had come here often to wonder at the sea, the monsters, the Vikings who had once invaded. Now, he stood motionless. James Sr. stood for a moment looking with his son at the waves crashing below the cliffs. Then he turned around and faced the countryside. James instinctively followed his father's lead.

"James, my boy, my son, I have often observed you looking out to sea, awe in your eyes, imagination dancing in your head. You were always intrigued by that which was beyond your grasp. I encouraged that in you for a boy must learn what lies in front of him before he can understand what lies behind him. Today, you are fifteen. Today, I have come here to look at our country together. My boy is becoming a man. Do you welcome this change?"

"Yes, father."

"As a man, you have to limit your imagination. Your reach must remain as it was, expansive, wondrous and inspiring. But you must use those qualities for that which is within your grasp. Are you ready to make that switch?"

"Yes, father," said James, now more confused than happy to be with his dad.

James Sr. spread his arms, heaved his chest and exclaimed, "My boy is a man today. He is the next generation of MacNessa. I proclaim him to this country, to my country, to his country – this is James MacNessa, son of sod and toil, son of lore and legend, son of kings and poets, son of warriors and gods."

James beamed as his father spoke, never having heard him speak of him thusly. He saw the pride in his father's eyes and his affection for him grew a hundred-fold.

"Son, you must follow me now. Trust me now."

With that, James Sr. turned and started walking to the edge of the cliff. He stopped at a large rock. James came up next to him and glanced over. There, close to twenty feet below was a ledge. His eyes popped out of his head and he looked up to his father.

From his waist, James Sr. pulled a rope, secured it around the base of the rock, and tossed it over. It landed on the ledge.

"Follow me."

And he was over the cliff's edge. James was in shock. His father, in some kind of ancient Irish regalia had just gone over the edge of a cliff… and told him to follow! James grabbed hold of the rope and looked over. His father was standing there, close to twenty feet below, looking up. James started to descend the rope and made his way tentatively down.

When he arrived at the ledge, his father patted him on the back and smiled. Then, with his other hand, he moved aside a hanging moss to reveal a small opening in the cliffside. James went in first.

Lighting a candle, James Sr. introduced his son to the ancient family hide-out. On the walls were shields and swords, statues and seals. As he scanned he saw what looked like three tunnel entrances. He walked around in wonder, scarcely believing that this was real. On the far side of the room was a large oak table with twelve chairs. His father had walked over and taken a seat. As James regained his composure, he was motioned over.

"James, your whole life, I have told you stories of the Ireland that once was and now lives in our legends and poems. Do you remember them all?"

"Yes, father. Every one."

"Good. Today, on your fifteenth birthday, it is my duty to inform you of who you really are, and what those stories really are. They are your family history, my son."

James sat there, wide-eyed and open-mouthed. Was he serious? All those stories of the Red Branch Knights, the famous saga Táin Bo Cuailgne, even, possibly, Cuchullain were all part of his family history?

"You see, Conor MacNessa was the great grandson of Rory Mor, the founder of the Rudrician line of kings and a monarch of Ireland. Conor, however, is the one who raised the family to prominence and had the foresight to prepare for the future. He was a great warrior and able leader, legendary on the battlefield. But he was also a patron of poetry and arts, and valued the intellect.

Now, as you are aware, scholars today categorize the early writings in Irish as Ogham. These slash marks, though loosely based on the Latin alphabet, have never been questioned and are undoubted as the first form of writing on the island. What they do not know about is Brythgoil.

In Conor's court, the great poet Ferceirtne held sway. As it happened, one day Néide came to court. He was the son of Ferceirtne's predecessor and he took it upon himself to try to take over the role. Clearly, an argument arose between the two. Conor decreed that there must be a public debate to settle the matter. A great number gathered to hear the debate between these two wordsmiths, as poets were greatly revered by even the lowest commoner. To the great dismay of public and king, the two argued in the ancient language of the scholars. Conor was outraged. No one outside the academic circles knew the language and those who did guarded it fiercely, even to death. Due to the traditional Irish honor of poets, no one had dared to question the linguistic isolation. Furthermore, many of the poets were protected by wealthy and ancient families who also wanted to maintain this separation from those of lower social rank. This day, the public outrage gave Conor both the support he needed to change the rule, and an opportunity he could not have possibly imagined."

"Did he kill the poets?" interjected James, his heart pounding.

"No, James, he did not. What he did was to abolish the use of the language in public, decreeing that it was no longer to be used by a few, but taught to all who wished to learn it."

"So, that's Gaelic?"

"No, it is not Gaelic. The Irish language, Gaelic, was then in a primitive form as the language of the average person. Conor was an adept politician and understood people; he knew that by throwing Brythgoil open to all, the common interest in it would decline after an initial spike. And he was correct. The public did not know, however, that before he announced the abolition of Brythgoil he had spoken to his poet Ferceirtne. He wanted to know from whence came the language and what the poet held in reserve. When the poet initially refused, Conor explained that after putting him to death, he would open the language to all. This was Ferceirtne's opportunity to explain the importance of the language, and save his own life.

The poet nearly lost his mind. His secret, the secret he was chosen to preserve, was about to be lost to a king courting public favor. He would have to betray the secret in order to save it. He sat down, asked the king to dismiss his guards, and began to speak. When he finished, Conor was the first Irishman on the island to become a Christian convert!"

"What?" shouted James. "How is that possible? Are you just making this up now?"

James Sr. laughed, because he had asked his father the same question. The pride he felt just a few moments before in the fields was intensified. His son was becoming a man, thoughtful and inquisitive. Should he go on? Or should he let his son have the childhood and adulthood he never had?

==

James smiled as he reflected. Remembering the pause of his father, and his own impatience to hear his father speak, he had no inkling of the change in his life the next words would contain. Or how he would then change the world.

===

Chapter Twenty-one: The Prince is Crowned
Dublin, Ireland

James Sr. paused and looked at his son. As his
father had changed his life, he was about to change his
own son's. Was it fair? Was it worth the price each of
them would pay? And on his death, with his failing
breath, would he have the courage to impart the
ultimate secret that had never been written, and never
been told outside of his blood? The moment of a few
seconds felt interminable and he almost lost his ability
to speak. Was he to continue; could he just tell his son
a story?
==

"Well, son, Ferceirtne explained to Conor the
true calling behind the poets of Ireland and why a few
ancient families protected them. It begins in the mists
of humanity, when the Tuatha deDanaan came to
Ireland and wrested control from the Firbolgs. The
battles were not only fierce, but cunning. Each knew
and valued the skills of their opponents. Upon victory,
the Tuatha deDanaan sought the origin of the Firbolgs'
weapons, especially the heavy sword, the *craisech*. A
boat of warriors was sent to Greek areas in search of
their homeland. A storm came, however, and the boat
was tossed about and finally crashed in the Middle
East. Most of the warriors died, including the leader,
Moytura. His young son was taken in by a kindly man
and raised as his own. That man was Noah. And
when the flood came, and Noah and his family were
saved, so, too, was Saer.
Saer knew of the conversation between Noah
and the Lord: mankind had 1000 years before the Lord

sent a sign, a Savior, that He was serious about the performance of mankind. At that point, humans would be given the understanding necessary for salvation. There would be a point of 2000 years in which mankind could seek to live out the Truth. Then, the Lord would come again. How or in what form was not revealed to Noah. So long as he lived out His word, he was safe. He was to foment the faith of the people and not worry about the Lord's plan. His duty was to teach the others, and maintain the calendar set down by the Lord.

The Calendar is essential to understand, James. You see, the Lord had already given his Chosen People 1000 years before the Flood. Now, they were to have 1000 more. But, it is not our calendar, it is the Lord's. It is not 365 days."

Seeing his son's confused face – a reflection of his own fifteen year old face long ago - he continued to explain that the calendar was exactly in tune with the cosmos. The years did not need a "leap year" because this calendar knew exactly when the year ended and when the next began; when each month precisely ended and when each season began.

"So," asked James, "Noah had the Calendar?"

"Well, at first, yes. Only Noah knew of its existence and only Noah knew how to calculate it. He did not, he could not, write down the Calendar. Remember, the Jews at the time were one of but a few learned peoples, and Noah feared discovery. He memorized how to form it and kept a labyrinthine system of marks on his door as a key.

Saer, through all of this, never forgot his island home. Though he loved his foster father and family, when he reached manhood, he informed Noah of his intentions to return home. He knew that the flood was intended to wipe out all, but hope remained that there were survivors in the Lord's mercy; that just as they were spared to repopulate the world, so, too, might there be survivors in pockets elsewhere. Thus, he returned to his homeland on a ship having agreed to spread the word of God to any living survivors."

"But," said James, "how could he do that? He was a child when he crashed. Even though he still wanted to return home, did he still remember how to speak Irish?"

"Now we get to the crux of the issue, son. No, he did not. He was forced to learn the language of Noah. If you think, however, of the Apostles after the Pentecost of Christ, you will understand what Saer could do.

The Lord had, in fact, sent a flood to the world. But, while the Hebrews and their descendents were the chosen people, all of the population of the world was not in the Middle East. In those areas where there were no people, furthermore, it made no sense to bring the rains. On top of which, indiscriminately killing is not what the Lord does. What He needed to do was to offer humanity a new start but also demonstrate his Covenant with His people. He brought the flood in all populated areas of the world. While He informed Noah of His plans, He sent signs to the other peoples. Signs they could interpret through their religious background which foretold of the coming of a messenger of the One, True God. For some it was a white dove after the flood. For others it was a fire in the distance. Each culture, each people, had their mystics interpret the signs.

As you know, Free Will allows people to come to God willingly. He does not want to interfere directly. The signs, however, allowed for a guidance that the people could choose to follow. Or choose not to. For the Irish people, the sign was two seemingly random arrivals on the island, separated by years, followed by a simple prophecy. You see, Noah's family was to be saved, but not everyone in the family was as good and holy as Noah. Some of them knew this and tried to escape. They did not know they would help the Lord's efforts. Bith, a grandson of Noah, and his daughter, Lady Cesair, sailed west to escape the flood waters. With them went Lady Cesair's son, Bith's grandson, Finntann. As they sailed, the Flood waters rose and capsized the boat. All succumbed except Finntann, who was still asleep in his bed. He floated, under God's protection, west unto Ireland. Upon his arrival, he could not communicate with anyone. The people were intrigued by his clothes and his language, his appearance and his ability to live on a bed in the sea. It took weeks, but finally Finntann was able to communicate that he had survived a flood of some sort and that his family had perished. The survivors of the Irish flood had mixed feelings. Could there have been a world-wide flood? Could a child survive such a deluge?

In the midst of the discussion, an old man came forth and offered to care for the boy, teach him to speak, teach him to read and write, and teach him a trade. This was followed by greater discussion, but at least the boy had a home.

The boy seemed incapable of learning anything

new. While he worked hard at simple tasks, and was nothing but amiable, he did not learn the language, he did not learn a trade. This greatly bothered the elders who felt there was something wrong with him and he should be sent back to sea. But the old man spoke on his behalf. He had come to them for a purpose. He had survived alone, in a bed, in tossing seas and endured hardships beyond compare. To send him off was base and without concern. In fact, he should be guarded by the community as a sign that even through the great assaults of nature, man can survive. The people agreed and the boy stayed. That was the first "random" arrival.

The second happened a few years afterwards. Saer had finally left Noah and his adopted family and sailed for his home. In their parting evening, Noah and Saer walked in the hills and meditated. Noah blessed Saer, hugged and kissed him as his own son. He was to carry on Noah's work, the divine message. In order to do that, Saer would need to be able to communicate with others. The Lord had given to Noah the linguistic ability to bring the animals on the Ark. So, too, was the Lord to give to Saer the linguistic ability to communicate with other cultures.

Noah took off a ring of wood and placed it on Saer's right hand. This ring housed the divine ability. It was also the key for the Calendar. Without it, all was lost. The Lord had imparted to Noah His desire that Saer should bring His wishes west. He would need the Calendar. Once the ring was on his finger, Noah was able to speak freely, to explain it all to him and to embrace him as a messenger of the Lord.

Saer was overwhelmed. He never expected

anything so great to ever happen to him. In fact, he looked at his life as a series of disconnected and troubling events. This united it all and enlightened him as to his purpose; he was a tool of the Lord, chosen amongst others to carry His Word. So shocked was he that it took a moment for him to realize Noah was not using Hebrew, or even Irish, but some third language he had never heard before. He was stunned. Noah smiled and explained the work of the Lord was conveyed in a new tongue, one he understood now with the ring. Noah called it Brythgoil.

Saer could teach it, but he could impart it only to those whose ears were open to learn. Furthermore, with the ring, he could communicate with any person. He truly was a messenger of the Lord.

And so, Saer left, jubilant. Along the way, he spoke to many peoples, landed in many ports, and was able to communicate with them all. He regaled them with his memories of the island at the far west of the known sea, of the people and the music. He ever spoke of the greatness of the Lord and His Mercy after the flood. In some places, he found converts, in others indifference to his message. But no one turned him away.

Finally, two years after departing, he landed in Ireland. His arrival brought murmurs and shock to the people. Was he not dressed as the boy from the sea? Did he not look like the boy? They scrambled and brought the boy to the new arrival – clearly they did not recognize the son of Moytura, he who left so many years ago. Finntann and Saer looked at each other, and after a moment, they recognized each other, and embraced. They knew the Lord had spared them.

Instantly, they began speaking and sharing experiences from the past few years. The people surrounding them were dumbfounded. How could two people, years apart, not knowing the language and customs of Ireland, land in the same place?

After many minutes, Saer paused, turned and spoke… in Irish! The people jumped back in fear. What? How? They were so confused several wielded their weapons. 'Wait!' shouted Saer, and he explained it all to them. His trip with his father, the crash on the shores, the family of Noah taking him in and his connection to this boy Finntann, the Flood and his return trip.

This was the work of the Lord, he explained, the One God who cares for His People. He was taken in by the Chosen people and sent here to share that blessing. The words that flowed forth from his mouth were honey to the ears, and the people were captivated. Saer knew that his message needed to be carried on after his death. He spent the next few years observing the people and identifying those with a genuine spirit. Once he knew the families, he approached each quietly and informed them of his true calling. Already respected and revered, the families needed little convincing. Saer took a few of the boys and girls from these families and instructed them in the message of God, and the language of Noah. The families protected them and encouraged others to do the same. This is the beginning of the Irish custom of respect and hospitality to poets and wise men."

"But how did he pick the families?"

"Ah, that James, is speculation. I don't know how he did that. Many assume he selected families of respect; with some means – if not wealthy outright; connected to, if not themselves, chieftains; and, as I mentioned, of genuine spirit.

Anyhow, Ferceirtne continued to explain to Conor that is was these families who protected the secret, who fomented good demeanor, who were the driving force behind the ancient laws – the Brehon Laws. He, Ferceirtne, was a direct descendant of Saer, and he was the keeper of the Calendar. To prove it, he showed his ring to Conor. It was not enough. Ferceirtne closed his eyes, touched Conor's ears, and spoke to him first in Hebrew, then Aramaic, then Greek – all languages Conor did not speak… yet he understood!

Conor jumped back, eyes wide, mouth agape and gawked at Ferceirtne. He believed.

Now, it happens, that just a few months before, the wise men of King Conor saw a sign they could not interpret. A white dove flew in front of the king's court in three circles, flew straight up and then, as it descended straight down, it burst into flames, falling on several people present. They were not burned, but felt energized as never before. The wise men called it an evil sign that peace would end, that the enemies were at hand and there were probably spies amongst them.

Ferceirtne pulled Conor aside later that night and explained this as the sign of the birth of Christ. The 1000 years had come."

"And Conor believed?"

"And Conor believed. And Conor struck a deal. Ferceirtne was to be the founder of a secret order. This order would no longer simply preserve

Brythgoil, but propagate it. The language was to be used among the royal family and select "friends". Conor explained that he felt the call, knew he was to be a messenger. As a conquering king, he could spread the word more quickly than a few wandering poets. The aim of the poet's work was the preservation of Brythgoil for the learned select, as well as the language, laws and culture of Ireland. Ferceirtne accepted and dove into his work instructing Conor and preparing a successor to carry on the information.

Conor, meanwhile, dove into his work constructing a plan for the future. As Rory Mor had risen to Ard Righ of Ireland, Conor, too, was ambitious. But he wanted more than Ireland, and he wanted it not just for himself, but for his descendents. Selecting his most trusted warriors, he included them on the plan, and made them swear a blood oath to never reveal their knowledge.

They decided that rather than fight each other, they could accomplish more together. They must not simply conquer men, but change their hearts. It would not be easy work. Men sometimes do not know what is best for their own good. They had to demonstrate, live out good lives to show man and to show the Lord that humanity was worthwhile. But those were difficult times. Conor recognized through his own human frailties that his ultimate success depended on how well his successors could deal with their own. First and foremost, Conor realized he needed comrades he could trust without a single iota of doubt. With his warriors, Conor convinced them that the short-sighted goal of wealth hindered their progress.

By dividing their wealth, they would be focused. He, as founder and king, was to be *primus inter pares*, first among equals, when it came to decisions and strategy.

They then went about scouring the land for isolated and difficult to reach locations. Once found, they made provisions for eating, sleeping, and general living. You and I are sitting now in our ancient hideaway, safe from all prying eyes and ears.

As for Ferceirtne, he could find no successor, and worried greatly. Furthermore, while others had had sons to carry on the Calendar, he was yet to be wed. Conor saw this as an opportunity to deepen and maintain his claim to *primus inter pares*, and offered one of his daughters in marriage. Once wed, even though he may never know the Calendar, the secret would become part of his lineage. The secret of the Lord would travel in his bloodlines, *our* bloodlines!"

===

Chapter Twenty-two: JT's Schedule
Santiago, Chile

JT left the embassy before midnight, hoping to leave the good impression intact. He had spoken to the biggest men in Chile, and in speaking to them, he heard names pass in casual conversation that he had previously heard only on CNN. His head was spinning as he left the building. Yet he knew he had made great connections, and the men appreciated seeing the face that would carry their information and files thousands of miles. He had made only one trip so far, nothing of importance really. All he had to do was drop a briefcase off in an office in Boston, hop back on the plane and fly back to Chile. Meeting these men, convincing them he was capable of more than being a simple errand boy, boosted his confidence. The night had been worth the risk, after all.

Back at the embassy, some others thought the risk was worth it, too.

"He is as you say, Gerardo, smart and intelligent, but he is simple. He has no pretension; he does not even hide his awe in sitting at this table. I like him."

Heads nodded agreement as Señor Ramón spoke.

"Let us take a closer look into his life, and make sure we are not the simple ones. We'll talk more in two weeks. *¿De acuerdo?*"

Again, heads nodded.

==

José Luis had spent some time trailing JT, watching him, looking for vulnerable spots in his schedule. JT kept himself busy, however. That worried José Luis. He knew that if JT was successful in his dealings with Gerardo, he would be trailed for certain. He might be under surveillance now, just as a precautionary measure. He had to find a way to communicate quickly, effectively and consistently.

Walking into the coffee shop that day and watching JT interact with Mariela had been a revelation. They had a simple interaction that could not be mistaken. No one would suspect anything unusual; the café was already a part of the routine. But, how?

==

Just a day after the embassy party, JT felt his importance rise when Gerardo called him at home. Not rugby this time, he was asking for a fourth for golf. Did JT play?

"Well, that depends, sir. Do you mean can I hit the ball, or do you mean can I hit the ball straight?"

"Worry not, my young man, I am more concerned with your social interaction today. You see, today I am golfing with the presidents of the largest publishing house in Latin America and the new director of the Asian and Latin American Trade Commission. They seem to think that the Latin American youth is nothing like his North American counterpart. I disagree. I see similarities on many levels, but they will not listen to me. I would like to show them firsthand how a youth from the States can fit so well into Latin America precisely because of his similarities. What do you say?"

What could he say? He went golfing.

It was unbelievable, but all week he felt that

Gerardo was seeking him out, asking his opinion, introducing him to all his contacts. It felt great. JT never realized how invigorating it was to converse with such a high level of motivated society. Had it not been for the simple things in his daily routine he might have let his ego take over his life. But getting an extra cup of coffee for the boss definitely reminded him daily that he was still an underling.

Tuesday has been a particularly good day with Gerardo taking the afternoon to show JT some of the sites in Santiago. While he had seen many of them already, Gerardo was able to take him into the basement of the Church of San Francisco, into the heart of the Cerro San Cristobal beyond the fountains, into the government section of La Moneda, and in the private rooms of the Museo de Arte pre-Columbiano. These were places not included on any tour.

Wednesday, when he walked into the café, he was on cloud nine. Mariela noticed immediately, and taunted him.

"How can you smile entering this shop? I thought you needed to see me to smile for the first time? Am I losing my charm?"

JT actually blushed at that. He was slowly becoming attracted to her; he was letting himself realize he was becoming attracted to her. Was there something between them?

Mariela smiled. She noticed the wheels spinning in his mind. She had let the same thoughts enter her mind weeks ago, but kept fighting if off as the musings of a silly girl and handsome foreigner. As a result, she had mixed feelings when she was asked to flirt more openly with JT because it was not about the flirting at all. True, José Luis (if that was his real name) had convinced her at the time that her actions would ultimately benefit JT. She also let herself believe him when he said JT would not be offended, and she let herself hope that if that statement was true, maybe, just maybe, JT would be willing to buy her a cup a coffee.

"Mariela, if you were losing your charm, would I ask you to have a cup of coffee with me every day?"

"Well, *mi guapito*, you have not yet asked me today, and so I am doubting."

"Mariela, *mi cafecita*, would you have a cup of coffee with me?"

Mariela handed a cup to JT with a cardboard sleeve.

"This cup I give you has a sleeve to protect your hands from the heat of the coffee. If you bring this very sleeve back tomorrow, I will have a cup of coffee with you, and I will write down my phone number on the sleeve. Now go, I have to work. I can't allow impish gringos to flirt with me all day!"

"*Hasta mañana*, then." And JT walked out to the office.

==

The man in the corner of the café never even lifted his head, but he watched as JT left. He then flipped his cell phone and made a call.

"Everything is clear. He is on his way to the office. We have nothing to worry about from him. *Ciao*."

==

JT arrived at the office and dove into his pile of work. While his time in Chile had been exciting, with moments of joy and moments of sadness – especially with Janey – he was just then on an upswing. Work was going well, he enjoyed his host family, his classes were interesting, and he might have a date.

He sipped his coffee, and smiled.

Gerardo walked into his office and pulled him into a meeting. JT was to do nothing but take notes this time, but, still, he was in another meeting. And take notes he did. He memorized the names of the people in the meeting, the main points of discussion, the main problem areas within those points, and his boss' opinions. He was not sure what he would do with it all, but he figured he should know it.

The meeting over, Gerardo offered to buy JT a drink. He wanted to know about next semester; what was JT going to do?

"Sure, I'd love to get a drink. Let me clean up my office, and I'll meet you downstairs."

JT ran back to the office, cleaned off his desk, and headed downstairs with the coffee cup in his hand. He slipped the sleeve into his front pocket, and tossed the cup into the trashcan near the lobby.

"So, JT, what will you do next semester? Would you consider staying here in Chile?"

"That's an inviting offer, but I am planning on going to Egypt next semester to study. And, my dean is expecting me to go there. We had some pretty long discussions, and I think if I changed my mind now, I would have problems when I returned to school."

Egypt? Is this too good? Gerardo's mind raced. The surveillance had shown nothing but a student working hard, studying and trying to enjoy himself in a new country. They had not been wrong yet, and of course he would check this young man's college assignment, so Gerardo opened the possibility.

"JT, you have been a great asset to us. And we hope to continue our relationship long after you leave my country. Are you interested?"

===

Chapter Twenty-three: When we are finished…
Santiago, Chile

Gerardo was the point man to check out JT and his life, his school and his plans. From everything he had seen since that first meeting on the rugby pitch to the embassy, he was convinced this young man was genuine. He did not even realize the level of people with whom he spoke at the embassy. JT's role as an assistant to him made his own enquiries relatively easy. By calling from his office and under the guise of "clearance to work for a visiting foreigner", most people were quite happy to give information. And the fact that JT was a sincere person had made people happy to talk about him. A few even gushed that they were so happy he was seeing good times, given his past; his past about which Gerardo was unaware, but which was quite beneficial to discover.

The surveillance time and again in Santiago showed nothing but a young man fully engaged in his life, his studies and his work with Gerardo. His routine was set, he followed it almost automatically. Any straying from it was generally traffic, or a sandwich shop, or the library. The closest things he had to a social life were either with his host family or flirting with the coffee shop girl.

Gerardo was dumbfounded. Not only was JT in Chile for the exact reasons he had stated, but he was there with literally no blood connection to the US. Nothing. If this kid died in a rafting accident in Guam, no one would raise a fuss. The school would pursue the matter, sure, but with zeal only in the beginning. With no one to follow up, and daily chores ever present, it would be shelved and soon forgotten.

It was time to call his uncle.

"*¿Y?*" said the uncle.

"*Es increíble*, but it is true what I tell you. This kid fits perfectly. We have checked, double checked and triple checked. His host family house is bugged and watched, he is watched and followed and his background is clean. Our friends in the States confirm his story there, too. We can use his services here and into the next year and then, when we are finished..." Gerardo's voice trailed off.

"*Sí*, when we are finished..." chuckled his uncle. "*Buénopo*, call him and tell him he is invited to the meetings. Tell him to be prepared, to be courteous, and to be alert. I will see you then, *mi sobrino. Bien hecho. Ciao.*"

"*Ciao, Tío.*"

Gerardo put down the phone and called JT into his office. He explained that in the next few weeks there would be several important meetings with some of the men he met at the embassy. JT made a positive impression on them and they wanted to see him again. But, he was to be working and not socializing.

JT beamed. He had impressed those men? Wow! He was beside himself with joy so much so that his reaction was genuine, and strong enough to help him forget momentarily that he would be working for two bosses in those meetings. Gerardo noted the reaction as he pressed for his secretary to come into the office.

"*¿Sí, señor?*"

Gerardo glanced at JT, who had taken a seat on the couch.

"Marisol, confirm the meetings for the next month, arrange my passport and flight to Shannon for May. Also, can you get me a *café con leche*? And JT, something to drink?"

"Huh? What? I'm sorry I did not hear what you just said." he mumbled.

Gerardo smiled. This was great.

"*Café*, do you want one?"

===

Chapter Twenty-four: MacNessa through the Ages
Ireland

James Sr. continued explaining to his son the role of the descendents of Saer. It happened over time and through careful observation. Conor was successful in marrying his daughter to Ferceirtne, but it turns out that his daughter only gave birth to daughters, three of them. After the third birth, Ferceirtne was beside himself with frustration and despair; he felt he had let down generations of his forebears. Though he loved his daughters, he felt his higher calling weighing on his shoulders. He went into the countryside to meditate.

Since his meeting with Conor, he had seen great changes in his life. His status and prestige in the community had risen. His circle of students shrank to a more focused and more energetic size. His personal life with Conor's daughter, he had to admit, left him fulfilled. But had he let his calling, his destiny fall to the side for temporal, carnal pleasures? Was he betraying his mission? Should he seek other women, any woman, who might bear him a son to carry forth the mission? He could not escape the inquisition he put upon himself. He was a more thorough examiner than any king could have brought before him.

He spent 40 days in the hills, wandering, seeking out the guidance he needed. The time away from his life left him feeling more relaxed, and more open to his calling, but he found nothing he could grab hold of in his travels. He returned with mixed feelings and resumed his life as advisor to the king, and motivator to his students.

Conor had been correct about the ability of a king to conquer and therefore set out the mission more quickly and effectively to the conquered. Nonetheless, the road was difficult. The old druids held great sway and their ability to seemingly manipulate and interpret natural events scared most of the people into submission. Thus, the important conquests were not quantitative so much as qualitative; they were able, in each kingdom, to sway one or two influential families. With each family, one of the more learned students of the school of Ferceirtne was placed. In this way, a steady network was built.

For many years, the secret society carried on the simple mission of maintaining the Truth and carrying on the tradition and history of the island. The work of Saer with prominent families long before had secured the public esteem of poets. In fact, poets had long been seen by the common people as almost more important than the nobles for their ability to entertain while preserving their history and their beliefs. The pragmatic ability to defend their homesteads kept the nobles and chieftains in power, but it was the poet who won their hearts. Great chieftains kept a poet in their court, sometimes several, and in so doing were able to win hearts as well. The strongest increasingly came from Ferceirtne's hut, carrying on the mission and regaling the crowds.

Throughout this time, Ferceirtne continued to struggle with his own mission as the leader of this secret society. What was he to do, actually? What were his students to do through the years. It was a happenstance observation which brought him clarity.

Over the years, his daughter became friendly with Conor's son, Padraig. He often saw them chatting together, and noticed, more than once, Padraig come calling on Moira for advice. And Padraig had gone through a series of "best friends", which seemed normal for a prince; one had to be careful whom one trusted. This day, Ferceirtne was reciting some lines of poetry on a hill when he noticed Padraig screaming and yelling at his most recent best friend. With a wave of his hand, he was dismissed. Padraig slowly watched as the friend departed, then turned and walked to a nearby hill to where his daughter was. Never quite certain of their relationship – was it friendly or romantic? – he was curious as to what he was witnessing. He watched as Padraig sat down and put his head in his hands, clearly exasperated. His daughter then sat in front of him, not to next to him as a lover would, and touched his hand, not his shoulder. Clearly, Padraig was not her lover. Then, a most remarkable thing happened, she lifted his chin, and stared into his eyes. She did not wipe tears, she did not comfort with her arms; she gave assent and strength through her eyes only. It stuck Ferceirtne like a charging bull; Padraig regardless of how many best friends he dismissed, had always come back to Moira. He would always come back to Moira.

Ferceirtne knew then the role his society was to play, and the king could not know this truth. In order to carry on the mission, they had to be reliable, consistent and continual. They had to become advisors to those in power. They had to remain when the kings were killed, or when power changed hands randomly. To an outside observer, this would be seen as a power grab. Clearly, to any king, who as a group were generally distrustful, nervous and wary of betrayal, this activity could not be tolerated. If this policy was discovered, they would be killed.

Worse, Ferceirtne could never explain that this was not a power grab. He realized he could never hope to carry out his mission if his future were left to the mercurial changes of temporal power. Nor could his students. They had to be beyond power, they had to shape their own destiny and, through it, the destiny of their people. The Lord was coming in time, their calling through Saer had been to make ready the people. It was not "listen to the kings". The great poet now saw his confusion: he was confusing the mission Conor had given him – basically at sword point – with that given to him from God. The secret society of Conor would work and, in fact, could be utilized toward his true mission. But the secret society would need to be a true secret society, one that sits behind the throne and whispers, not on the throne screaming.

The realization repeated in his head that if kings knew that they were planning anything on such a scale, the poets would be killed. For, despite the love of the poets by the people, kings were kings and could always find a way to fulfill their wishes.

In order to communicate this revelation to his students, Ferceirtne sent word that at the great festival of Lughnasa, all the poets from his school would have a meeting. The festival of Lughnasa was a huge success. Ferceirtne was even able to have Conor enforce the secrecy of the meeting. By claiming he was hoping to gather information to maintain the king's central role, Conor eagerly set up a concert and invited all the royalty to attend. Who would dare refuse the *Ard Righ*, the High King? Ferceirtne was free to communicate with his students, who were quickly becoming his partners.

It was here the basic framework which still stands 2000 years later was created. They laid out the network, the system of communication and the ultimate goal of making the people ready for the coming of the Lord.

The most important rule was communication. The language they inherited from Saer had to be more closely guarded, even from kings. Though many through Conor's request had been instructed in it, the poets began to diminish the importance, at least with the kings. Appealing to the pride of the kings, it was easy work. By calling it the language of the peasants, no king wanted to continue speaking it, or even acknowledge its existence. Eventually, only the poets knew the language, as had been the case before Conor. Better for the new society, people forgot about the language and it was as if it never existed. The second improvement was the more stringent guidelines for inviting a student into the society. While family was still the strongest factor, other characteristics played a large role: intellect, sense of purpose, trustworthiness, analytical skills. Thirdly, an active pursuit of tact was encouraged. The only manner to ensure their mission was to be able to act without their respective kings or leaders comprehending the actual role play. Fourth, Ferceirtne solidified Conor's *primus inter pares* in regard to his own role. They were equals, but they needed a guiding light, someone to make ultimate decisions in tough times. Given his ability thus far, this was easily agreed upon. The final guideline was perhaps the riskiest, in terms of discovery, betrayal and greed. They were extending the idea of primus inter pares to money and wealth. As Conor had convinced his warriors to fight more for each other than for gold, Ferceirtne convinced his poets to supplant their positions and build their own network of wealth and security.

In the beginning, while Conor's network was functioning well, Ferceirtne simply piggy-backed his students and swept forward with Conor. His students were soon the chief advisors to most of Conor's allies, both his own warriors and his regal counterparts in nearby kingdoms. The work itself was difficult. Druids, wise men, seers and any embedded power fought tenaciously to maintain and increase their position. As their society, their work was subtle, with hints and simple comments planted in the kings' minds. Never once did a poet bluntly state that the One, True God would come to erase the pagan Celtic gods. Never once did a poet question the polytheistic views of a king. Instead, strong attributes were praised. Devotion to one god, regardless of each king's personal favorite, was used to foster the belief that one god had more power than others. Their one god, who the poets knew to be the One God, always had their beneficent characteristics highlighted and praised in song, in the recounting of a victory or a miracle.

Confidence played a role unforeseen by Ferceirtne. As a result of their history and sense of purpose, each poet acted decisively and firmly. In contrast, the Druids generally advanced through the fear of the people and their inability to explain natural events or losses in battle. The poets hinted at these in advising the kings, wondering aloud how any king could stake his future on the whims of a fearful group, unsure of why the "gods" were hostile or kind. As word of this difference and its effect on the kings spread through the network, each poet made steady advances.

No one questioned Ferceirtne. He carried on consistently in his work, never trying to advance, never downplaying the work of his poets, never straying from the mission. This was clear and known and emulated by all. The kings increasingly came to rely on them as almost co-regents. But Ferceirtne's steady practice of allowing the king to continue in vocalizing the laws and mores fostered the strength in them all.

At home, meanwhile, he watched his daughter and Conor's son and wondered if she had the ability to become a poet. He investigated with a few political questions, idly mentioned over dinner. Then relationships were examined, and history and finally, he began to ask her to entertain the household after dinner. She was able to recite history and poetry, mythology and tradition. And her father smiled. Conor's son would one day be king and he was already being groomed in the classical skills. The people loved him, and he had the potential to rule well for generations.

Ferceirtne began to train and educate his daughter. Other poets watched. Would he accelerate her education because she was his daughter? Would he impart the secret hastily? The great poet knew this, and understood the implications of his actions. The manner in which he conducted his daughter's education and possible entrance into the society would set the pattern and literally make or break the success of it. The zeal of his mission, the pride of a father, had to be restrained if the society was to succeed. He spent five years educating Moira in the arts of history, poetry, rhetoric and language. Then, he spent three more years challenging her, questioning her, implicating her in scandals and plots to observe how she extricated herself from trouble.

After eight years, after numerous consultations and countless hours analyzing and preparing her mind, he took her on a retreat into the countryside. Moira knew it was meant to be an important time, but she was not sure of what it was her father was doing. He waited three days to tell her. To Ferceirtne's surprise, she did not exhibit great shock. She had anticipated her role was to elevate in importance and she trusted her father, whom she knew to be a brilliant advisor to the king. She understood her role in relation to Padraig even before he commenced explaining the plans for the society.

===

Chapter Twenty-five: The Risks of Advising

Moira returned from her countryside trip without any outward appearance of the changes that had taken place. Her role elevated her status in the network, both because of her own efforts and the precautionary steps taken by her father. Nonetheless, she felt no pressure, since her role was the same as the rest – work toward the mission. As an informal advisor to Padraig she continued to expand the horizons of the society.

As men are wont to challenge for power, Conor was frequently besieged by those who knew not of his role with his own society. In their political intrigues, they often approached Padraig appealing to his pride and ambition to accede to the throne. Moira continued to advise, suggesting that he wait and bide his time. For if these men were willing to overthrow his father, how long would they wait to overthrow him? By way of such wise counsel, besides convincing him of her worth, she learned who in the area had power and who was applying pressure. Through the network of poets, each knew what was changing and who would soon see power.

The reality of life is that not every leader has the education or skills to lead. Not every king or queen can take eight years to master their craft, as the poets did for their protégés. With human nature super-ceding the power of kings, the poets learned to ingratiate themselves with strong potential leaders. It was a complicated task, learning to maintain a loyal relationship with the king while winning over new leaders and all the while seeking to further their mission in the eyes of all who held power.

As times changed and the governments became more complex, the poets traveled and lectured each other so that they could continue to move forward as one group. As a result, they were able to navigate the tricky process of emerging complex government and made easier accepting a "position" in the government while remaining the nearest advisor to the seat of power.

At times, the intrigue became too much. Kings or queens would snap and behead an advisor, or lash out and scream conspiracy. Occasionally, a poet would succumb to the temptation of power and money and seek out the throne. All the while the society watched and waited. Their discipline allowed them to wait until action was necessary, if it was. In a few cases, having the poet as king fostered their aim and promoted education of the people of the value of living a life prepared for the coming.

All the while, Conor, ignorant of Ferceirtne's renewed sense of mission, continued on with his own goals and objectives. His society slowly began to unfold, however. The mission he sold to his warriors slowly drifted from their central aim. They still had to fight and bleed, to support their families and, in many cases, clansmen in both good harvest and bad. The reality of life, with its need for food, shelter and protection, was more pressing than a supposedly heavenly coming of a single god some absurd amount of years in the future. Even appealing to their temporal greed of forming an oligarchy echoed hollow in empty bellies.

Conor struggled to maintain it, to win victories

and thereby to demonstrate with physical objects the value of spiritual unity. He tried structure and discipline, arranging regular meetings and a system of checks and balances. It was futile effort. One by one, the warriors sought new alliances, fought amongst themselves and left Conor alone.

Conor had a long reign and his people loved him. By most accounts, his was one of the better reigns in the beginning history of Ireland. At his death, though, he felt like a broken man. When the in-fighting had begun, he had not yet informed his son Padraig of the society. Then, it was too late. Over the years he never decreased his faith in the mission, and was gratified to see Ferceirtne continue on by his side. He begged him never to let on to his son what the truth was unless he was certain that he could accept and struggle for it alone, as he had done. Ferceirtne agreed.

Conor never dreamt that the mission would continue on through the poet, or for that matter, through his poet's daughter, the now official advisor to his son. Nevertheless, it was his only beacon of light knowing that the advice he received from such a man as the poet might continue on to his son, the king of his island.

Ferceirtne was genuinely grieved when Conor died. He admired the man, he trusted the king, and he knew he could not explain his work through the years. Upon his death, he assumed the secret location for his locale. Others in the society began to assume those of their leaders; it was easy as most were left dormant as Conor's network dissipated.

===

Chapter Twenty-six: The Secret is Out
Isla Negra, Chile - 1970

On a blistering cold night, two poets were chatting by the sea. One was published and beloved by his country men and cherished by his country women. The other never published a single word. They were drinking pisco sours and smoking, enjoying the sea and the cold.

Like most writers in the country, they had often met in the streets of Santiago, in the hidden bars and cafés off the La Avenida Libertador Bernardo O'Higgins. Theirs was a world of smoke and alcohol, lust and passion, politics and philosophy. They wore capes and berets, walked with canes. They refused manual labor but praised the working man of Chile. Though married, they often awoke in the arms of different women. Their wives often did the same. It was bohemian, basic, base and carnal. They led the poet's life as they thought it should be.

Of pressing importance was the changing tide of Chilean politics. The country was in an economic tailspin and the people were losing themselves and, consequently, the country was losing its soul. This had been the topic of all debate: what should they do? What could they do? Some, like Victor Jara, brought music and poetry to the people to cheer them and encourage them through the tough times. Others, like this guest to Isla Negra, hinted at more aggressive action.
==

They had been talking already for hours. The

great poet and Auggie knew each other for years, though they had chosen quite different paths. Neruda was open and loud with his views, penning poems as if breathing them. Auggie came from a lesser upper class family, and had chosen the "more traditional" path of a soldier, and was advancing well. Importantly, he was an expert at covert work, able to manipulate and somehow remain loyal to his friends.

He was approached in the 1960's while defending an oil drill from striking and violent workers. Invited to a dinner as a "thank you", he arrived with his officers and finished the meal alone with Octavio Ramón de Mojica. Mojica followed the procedure for imparting information and possibly extending the final invitation. Auggie had no idea he was being watched, inspected and researched. His responses were genuine, he was loyal, and he could be trusted. After a year, he was introduced to several other prominent Chileans. After two years, the invitation was extended... and accepted.

He soon learned the entire mission and the goals of the society. Such a goal, lofty and noble, inspired him, filled him with a euphoria he never would have imagined. All his life, his struggles, his successes, made sense to him; destiny was grooming him to bring his people to a Salvation they dare not dream. That he should help usher it in was a blessing. As a result, he did not feel proud or elevated above his comrades. So, when he was told others from his country must be recruited, he was not slighted. To the contrary, he began his search in earnest, seeking out countrymen with gifts from the stars. That criteria indicated to him one man, one Chilean, one friend.

When he approached his council, they were not pleased. Sure, they knew the man, and they knew that he truly loved Chile. He would desire similar ends for the country and its people. But they knew he saw the end result successful only through his version of the world. But Auggie pressed his case, and finally, the council relented and gave him permission to speak, but once only, and with certain conditions.

Auggie let the night between friends proceed as it should, between friends. His business could wait. He enjoyed spending time with his friend, his eccentric, brilliant and adored friend. The sadness of turning the discussion serious almost turned down the lights.

"*Mi amigo*, I must take this moment to talk to you about something dear to our heart, Chile. But, *buénopo*, what we discuss you may not repeat. I ask you as a friend, let these words pass no further than our ears. I beg you for the poet can only control the words he writes, not how people read them."

There was a glance, a nod, and what could be taken as an introduction to a persuasive argument.

The rejection was almost immediate. His friend gave his heart to the people and "the people's voice" – Marxism. He saw no other way than through the workers themselves. He barely tolerated an argument and the only reason he was civil or even courteous was because his opponent happened to be his friend. Both being tenacious, however, the argument was not simply a few minutes. They enjoyed each other's point of view simply because they each agreed that the end was worth the argument, was worth the struggle.

Unfortunately, Auggie was not an expert in concealing his emotions from his friends, especially in emotional arguments. His friend sensed there was something lurking behind his voice, something not being spoken on purpose. Their common goal would lead them down different paths.

Auggie was frustrated. His friend loved his *país*, his Chile. Could he not make him see the Truth about to arrive on the shores of this very beach?!

"*Mi amigo*," he said, "*te hablo por cariño*, I do not have to be here. Receiving permission to come here was a difficult task in and of itself. Your views are not hidden. Coming here was seen as a fool's errand, but one I know you not only need, but deep down, desire."

"*Y tú*," responded the great poet Pablo Neruda, "are welcomed here as a friend, dear and beloved to me as the ocean waves. Let me tell you what a fool's errand is: it is turning your back on your people, it is pretending that an imported culture and ideology will work here in the Andes. The people here are of the earth, they have the resilient spirit of the Mapuche in them. It was a fool's errand 400 hundred years ago to come here for Pedro de Valdivia, and the Indians of the south still prove him a fool today, resisting the government."

"Of the same land are we, Pablo, this you know. The rainy south and the arid north are joined by the spine of the Andes. The blood of de Valdivia mingles with the blood of Lautaro. We are one body, and this is why we are here. The past is no more. To pretend we can hold onto it is like, is like saying we can hold onto the air. It can not be. Look even to our

Mapuche, fiercely holding onto their heritage, their version of history. Noble? Proud? *Sí, claro*. But what do they accomplish?"

The placid poet sipped his drink, looked at his friend, and turned to the sea. As the waves crashed on the beach, they felt the sea air mist over them, bathe them.

"Do you feel that, Auggie? By standing here we are covered, covered in sea air, in salt mist, in the mists of time and in the history of our land. We are not simply Chileans, we are Americans. We can not forget that the water which washes us now also washes our brothers and sisters in Perú, Ecuador, México, all of *América del Sur*. We can not, we must not, forget that. That, too, is a fool's errand."

"Pablo, listen to me, please! I ask again, what do the Mapuche accomplish by continuing on with a struggle more romantic than realistic? The world sees the "noble savage" of Rousseau without seeing their daily life of poverty, squalor, and fear of progress. They see Native American without seeing *América*. We will not forget the past, but we can not, we will not, stop the future. Those of us on the cusp of both the masses and the élite have a unique opportunity to save Chile. Even above our *vecinos sudamericanos*, we have an opportunity to bring to the people a better existence. But we must act, we can no longer let our words suffice. Now is the time."

"Now is the time. Indeed." replied Pablo.

He sipped his pisco and looked at his friend.

"Interesting that people have been saying that for so long in so many struggles, that it loses its meaning. José Martí thought it was the time; he put down his pen, and then put down his life. He entered a fight because he forgot it was a struggle. What did he accomplish?"

The reference and its message were not lost on the poet. Neruda's friend looked at him, with a touch of regret and sadness mingled with relief. He wanted Neruda, his *compadre*, to join him almost as much as he wanted him to resist and stay true.

"*Mi amigo*, I must tell, as I told you before we started our, *pues*, *nuestro discurso*, that you must not mention this night to anyone. It is beyond even me, even you. You see, it is not us we worry about, you and I; we know what we do and what we risk. But those we love, well, ..." and he trailed off, almost embarrassed to even have to think about the thought.

Pablo looked at his friend, drank him in, swirled him about his eyes and then poured himself into his friend. This was it. It was a moment neither could forget, but which neither could let restrain them. No further word of either persuasion or denial was necessary.

They stood there together for many minutes, sipping their drink of history and letting the smoke of their destinies swirl round their heads.

"I will miss you, *mi poeta*."

"And I, you, Pablo. But we do not say *Ciao*. To you, and to me, it is *A Dios*. Adiós."

==

Neruda could not let the conversation leave his mind. He flipped it over like a river stone in his hand, caressing it, rubbing it, trying to bleed it for more information. In just a few hours his friend had shown him years of work. But what could he do? He was not worried for himself in regard to his friend's guarded warning. Those he loved, however, knew not of the meeting and the violent storm about to descend on Chile and uproot its soul. Could he stop it? Did he *want* to stop it? Was the *gringo* Jefferson correct – did democracy have to be watered in blood now and again? Was it worth the price to simply sit idly by, to put down his pen even if he did not pick up another weapon?

As he pondered his dilemma, he continued on with his current work, his *Odas*. As it happened, this gave him an opportunity to warn the people without telling them. And so he wrote and wrote, he explained the fury of the storm to come, how it would tear trees from the ground and lash the mountainside and deluge the countryside, soaking everything in its path. But, so the people would understand, he painted the storm as temporary, not wanting or even able to cause lasting harm to this environment, this their Chile. Rather, like the great Deluge, it would refresh the spirit. The soul of Chile, like the leaf swirling down to the earth after seeing the inner depths of the furious storm, would return to the land and stay long after the storm left. No storm, no violent outburst, could affect the Chilean soul. This was his message, this was his *Oda a la Tempestad*. Would his people see it?
==

Several people did see it, and knew the message was out beyond their control. That could not be. It must not be. Traditionally, one answer sufficed to keep the secret secure. However, they could not touch the poet; they knew it and it gnawed at each member of the Chilean council. If this man disappeared, no Chilean would sleep until he was returned and, even then, he would still become a martyr for their cause. Questions would be asked, and some weaker members might collapse. No. They needed to send him a message, a signal, that next time he wrote a poem, he might not finish the last line.

The society had lasted through the years, and so when the idea arose of a way to send that signal to the poet, one phone call was enough to arrange it all. From one *hispanoparlante* to another, from one *poeta* to another, the message was sent. The target was quite a welcome target. For several years, his government had been watching him and was irritated by his inflammatory remarks, essays and poetry. The people were drawn to him, and the society watched carefully. With two World Wars and countless skirmishes, their skill and ability to remain beyond temporary politics had been tested in this century, true, but they had continued onward. This poet, however, was smart, inquisitive and relentless. His questions were becoming too pointed, too accurate. The phone call was enough to jolt them out of their malaise and take quick, decisive action. That it would benefit the society in another chapter was simply a bonus.
==

When word reached Pablo, it was devastating. His dear friend, his colleague, his fellow poet, was a hero in his mind. To have him die an ignoble death was to refuse the value of his life.

Worse, he understood all too well that it was his actions which precipitated the assassination. The manner of death, obscure to outside onlookers, was like a physical poem to him. His words about a storm in Chile brought thunder down in Spain and killed his friend Federico. He had taken a risk, and Federico lost.

He no longer hinted at what his friend told him. His struggle would not end, but this battle tactic would be fought no more by him.

==

Auggie never learned of Pablo's decision to follow his advice, albeit after an attempt. Those who read the poem could not tolerate any information leak. They handled the one leak, and knew it was effective. But that leak was initiated by Auggie. He had to be dealt with just as swiftly. Unfortunately, that decision was not as easy to make, and one phone call would not bring it about. Rather, the meeting was heated and impassioned. They knew Auggie had dedicated himself to the society and their cause. But his personal passions drove him to a friend. They were slightly culpable as well, they admitted, for letting him persuade them. Ultimately, however, they agreed that his passions and trust in his friends may again surface and the next friend may not be a poet. It had to be done. He had betrayed the mission.

Auggie was a well connected man. As a military officer, he had many connections, and with the covert US presence in Chile, he had an international presence. S. Timothy was a CIA operative in Santiago, both advising and monitoring the Chileans, and he had come to know Auggie pretty well. In fact, they often had a drink together in a little out of the way spot in one of the more rundown sections of town, *El Como Como*. It could be that as espionage agents themselves they were paranoid, but they figured no one would follow them there or even realize this was their chance to unwind and not think at all about work.

It was on one of these nights when the assassin hit. Auggie was leaving work with his bag and stopped at the café on the corner. His murderer was someone he knew from the society. He paid a kid to "bump into" him accidentally. Furtively, he placed a poison in his coffee while Auggie yelled at the youth. Then he casually said hello and chatted while his coffee sat on the counter long enough to absorb the powder. The powder was designed to strike a half hour after it was in the system. Auggie's dead body would be nowhere near his office or home and, therefore, any enquiry would be centered away from them, too.

Everything went according to plan. A half hour later just as Auggie stepped off the Metro and onto the street in front of El Como Como, he fell to his knees. He knew. He knew and the knowledge gripped him in fear. As he went down, his eyes locked with S. Timothy who saw him through the window. He knew the look, and rushed outside wondering what Auggie had done to be assassinated.

"Amigo," he cried. "*Me muero, me muero y no sé por qué.*"

"Calm down, Auggie, you're not dying, you'll be okay, just breathe. Breathe."

"Listen to me, listen!" gasped Auggie.

His breathing was strained now and he had no strength.

"Listen. There is a group, a group that did this to me. I can't believe it, they have betrayed me. They do not even know that they are about to be betrayed. The fools. The blind fools! The goal of MacNessa is not the goal of the Chilean MacNessa. The little General, he wants it all for himself. He does not care about the Coming. MacNessa, MacNessa must be... must be... MacNessa..." and with that, he slumped and died in S. Timothy's arms.

There was no time to grieve. A few onlookers were watching and so he started to scream for an ambulance. He jumped up and walked into the bar and indicated there was a commotion out front, everyone should go and help. They did, and he quietly slipped out the back door and disappeared. No one even remembered seeing him there.

S. Timothy criss-crossed the city in taxis, micros, the Metro, on foot. He needed to think. He knew about the little General, and he knew what was in the works. He knew that Auggie was close to him. But what was MacNessa? What must be protected? Who else did Auggie know? With what other group was he involved... and why did they kill him!?

He mentioned not a word to anyone for weeks. He barely trusted anyone in the city. A few weeks later he was due back to DC for a little R&R, and when he landed, he called his old mentor. He trusted him and knew he would have some insight.
==

"You sounded a little frantic on the phone, there, S. What's up?" asked Peter Blood casually.

"Is it safe here, Pete?"

"Of course it is. The office is bug free."

"Good. Listen to this."

He explained everything about his time in Santiago, but focused particular attention on the last few weeks and Auggie. When he mentioned the word MacNessa, Pete visibly winced.

"Damn it to hell. It might just be true."

===

Chapter Twenty-seven: Naming and Damnation
France, 8th Century

The single greatest threat to the Secret Society came in the 8th century, just as Charlemagne was rising to power. Charlemagne had unified a country and a people and gave hope to many that the dark times, the fractious times, of the previous few centuries in Europe were coming to a close. His reign was hope that Europe would find peace.

Charlemagne himself was very desirous of such an outcome. To achieve his ends, he sought divine inspiration. He sent emissaries all over the known world seeking holy objects, objects touched – or purportedly touched – by Jesus, Mary, the apostles or anyone remotely associated with the early Church. Already a thriving business, the relic business exploded, with hucksters and frauds finding a ready market; if the great Charlemagne wanted these so, too, did even the lowest commoner. Men became rich overnight, men were murdered, wives were duplicitous and children were spies. In the process, a decree was issued which had the greatest relics reserved for Charlemagne. This meant his advisors were essential to weeding out the frauds.

The Society had worked quietly for years and had been able to sidle up to Charlemagne just before his ascent, so he trusted these advisors. He saw them as pure, untouched by his acquisition of power and wealth. His two main advisors were of the Society, and so they were his last line of interference. As a result, they were able to command quit a hefty bribe for access.

As this was beginning, both accepted the money but maintained their frank opinions with Charlemagne. Eventually, the money and temptation increased to such a degree that it overwhelmed them and their advice to the king became poor, shortsighted and sloppy. The king noticed. He called his private guard and had them watched.

Their money grubbing was obvious and within a day Charlemagne called a private meeting with his two advisors, his guard and his sword.

The meeting was quiet. Charlemagne knew they knew the purpose of the meeting. Jean-Luc, the younger and less experienced, started to speak. The clear words were mission, future, God, secret, network and society. Edouard shot him a glance that shut him up, but these had been uttered. He feared this young man had just betrayed seven centuries of work.

Charlemagne, meanwhile, picked up the sword, walked to Edouard, and drove the sword through his chest.

"You were saying?" he said to Jean-Luc.

Eyes wide with horror and fear, Jean-Luc could not speak. He knew he would die. Edouard had been with Charlemagne for years; he was trusted and known to all as Charlemagne's man. And without hesitation, he was killed. Everything in Jean-Luc's life came into stark contrast in his head. His fear of death was now gone, it was his fear of the secret which now compelled him to act. Despite his recent greed, he knew he had to protect the secret, or else his life – temporal and eternal – was worthless. He had to extricate himself from this without betraying all. Yet, he knew that their deaths and the news of their deaths would be carried far and wide. He had started to make a mistake, and Edouard saved him with his life. He had to correct it. He had to assure the Society that all was safe. He had to choose his language carefully. He had to choose his death carefully.

"Your highness, I beg of you, forgive our, er, my actions. I have always acted out of a sense of duty. I am bound by my Lord and Protector."

Jean-Luc edged away from the king and began to pace the room. Did the king notice the words? What was he to do? Dare he fight the king? What about the fire? The window? If he were somehow kept alive they would torture him. Could he cope with torture?

"Edouard and I have erred. Temporal rewards have jaded our view; they have taken me off the path of righteousness. I must atone for my sins."

His words, spoken slowly and with great care, were being noted by the guard, who was watching this pacing man, prepared to defend his king at the slightest provocation. Were these words his warning? Would he attack? His ears were sharp.

"Well," said Charlemagne, "how do you propose to do so? Tell me what I want to know!"

"I can assure you, sire, that I have given my life in the name of the Lord, God, for the good of the Kingdom."

He bowed, looked at the guard clutching his sword, and at his king. Then he turned and jumped out the window, falling to the stone below.

He was correct. News of their deaths, and the words Jean-Luc spoke, were spread far and wide. While Charlemagne, a unique king but also still a king, suspected a hostile society working against him, he was never able to prove it. He spent money and manpower, all for naught. The commoners took the deaths and the words as proof that the advisors felt slighted by the mistrust of their king. The Society understood all, and bowed their heads in thanksgiving.

===

Chapter Twenty-eight: The Middle East Connection
Ireland

The story, the family history, James heard from
his father astounded him, but it was not that simple.
James had to memorize the story told to him. He kept
inquiring as to the full extent of the story, and his
father always replied that he would tell him more
when he had memorized what was already related.
And so, over the next years, piece by piece, the full
story was revealed of the Society, the organization,
and their role in history.

James Sr. delighted in the time with his son.
The words coming from his mouth were not his own,
yet they danced off his tongue, tickled even his ears
and filled storyteller and listener with wonder and awe.
To bring the story to life, father took son across the
island, highlighting the locations of decisive moments
in their history, explaining the significance of
monuments, ancient and mysterious to the Society.
All the while he taught him the language that had been
passed down to him from his father, and from his
father and from his father, making a connection 2000
years old. It was only in moments of quiet, inspired
by the magnitude of an event in the story or the reality
of seeing the ancient holy lands in person, that James
Sr. felt a tinge of sadness. He could never fully shake
it, but easily enough with his son there he could ignore
it successfully.

He was shaken from one of these moments by
the penetrating stare of his son. Sitting on the great
stone of swirls protecting the entrance to Knowth,
James Jr. had been alternately gazing at the

countryside and the massive formation.

"Father" said the boy, "I wonder why it is that such a great feat of human engineering would fall victim to disuse and then a public amnesia. I can't understand it, even in the face of the arrival of St. Patrick. It just does not make any sense!"

"Well, let's review it all again."

Most people know the story of Patrick, the Patron Saint of Ireland, who was of Italian origin and English lands. He was captured by pirates from England, sold to a king in Ireland, escaped, converted and saw a vision to return to Ireland, the land now in his blood and soul, in order to convert his fellow countrymen. Criss-crossing the island, he converted thousands. The interesting twist is how he was able to do so in a land steeped in mystery, where druids foretold everything and had the ear of every king.

From the outside, the method was ingenious enough: find a young, pliable noble from a good family and convert him. Continue to have the people revere the king and not impugn the druids. Build support slowly. Then as the numbers have increased and more and more people of the king are vocalizing their newfound belief, have the noble introduce the great prophet – the humble servant of Christ! – to the powerful king so that he might explain the benefits of embracing Christianity instead of driving a wedge.

And the common folk, oh they were easy to convert. The basic message of the druids was fear and darkness, human sacrifice, hardship and blood; whereas the Lord in His Love for mankind offered His Son as the last sacrifice so that mankind may have peace, joy, and light in their lives.

"And that is fascinating, father, but why abandon these sites? Why not, like most other things 'pagan' reassign meaning? Like All Hallows Eve?"

"You are missing the key point, my boy. You are forgetting the Society. Why do you think Patrick was permitted to breath one minute past the first druid complaining to a king? Why was he permitted to take the people from their religion and mystics, from their traditions and myths? It is because the Society knew he was coming, they knew he was going to win people with the message. It was the same message of the coming of the Lord!"

"So, they talked to him?"

"Oh no, they could not do that. For this conversion of Ireland to work, they knew Patrick had to be the driving force, and that he could never know. But, if they were not whispering in the kings' ears about the druids, and how easily they were frightened, and how their wisdom and divining was unable to provide them an answer to Patrick, the kings would have had him killed. This Ireland was savage, bloody, and fierce. Discussion was not an option in the face of a threat. The Society persuaded the kings to let him stay, watch him, see what he does. All the while, they were themselves slowly converting the kings. Thus, when it was time to be Christian, they were there but in name only and Patrick found converts at the ready."

"But what about these sites?" demanded James Jr.

"Well, son, these sites were great and mighty, known far and wide. The mystery surrounding their origin served the Society well. Even the druids were unsure of their original purpose. When it came to celebrate the Christian Mass, Patrick was wise enough to simply build new edifices of worship without attracting any attention to the sites. He told his followers not to make a scene and thereby remind people they were leaving behind the traditions of the fathers. They were to keep them excited about their own lives and futures while celebrating the souls of the forefathers. Eventually, time and abandonment erased the glimmer of druidical heritage. The sites became grazing lands, settlements and then of no notable value through the ravages of time and forgetfulness.

But the Society knew the sites held a spirit of the people and even though forgotten – or maybe because of it – they were perfect as central meeting locales. Even better, the Society found a hidden tunnel system connecting many of the sites. Probably escape routes in time of war, they now served as entrances hidden from common view. Often as not, they looked like small hills or dirt piles next to trees. In Ireland, with so much open land, no one suspected anything of another man walking around the fields. They would never realize that the hidden tunnels and carvings were central to the future of the world!"

Father continued to explain to son that the meetings of the Society were never discovered, nor were the tunnels under the great sites, by either the people or Patrick. Here, disciples were selected to lead expeditions in all directions. The main cause of concern to the Society in the beginning was the change of demeanor of an Irishman. Whereas previously associated with the battle face-painted, screaming warriors of the recent past, these new emissaries were overtly quiet and demure. Would they be believable to kings and princes as loyal advisors, or would they be suspected because of the unexpected change?

After the death of Charlemagne, as Europe fell into darkness, the mission of the Society was aided by the general proselytizing Irish spirit. Following the example of Patrick, monks set out by the hundreds and thousands to convert their fellow man to Christ. With so many Irish monks roaming Europe, the few Society members were not unusual. Their "inspired" wisdom further ingratiated them to kings who trusted them as men of God and not greedy mortals. The system of monasteries with Irish abbots throughout Europe became one of the best networks of travel not just for the Catholic Church and its adherents, but also for the Society, which used it freely and with ease.

Also with the death of Charlemagne, the rise of Islam loomed on the horizon of Europe. The Society was calm but pragmatic about the possible shift in temporal power. After all, they believed in the One, True, Imbrahamic God, the same God for Islam. Through the monasteries and the network of information, they learned the theology of Islam and the language, the culture and the customs, even the look and the smell of the rising religion. The members realized that the world was changing, and in order to continue with their mission, they would need to inculcate themselves with the Mohammedans. And they did. It took many years of attempts and many different tactics, but finally a few were accepted as converts. Their wisdom was soon obvious and the imams accepted them as advisors.

Their obvious physical differences made them immediately recognizable to the people around them, and only their acceptance by the imams kept them alive. Consequently, communication through the monasteries to the Society was, for these members, terminated. They were isolated in a foreign culture, hostile to the Catholic Christian religion. Only through their training and faith could they continue the struggle of the Society.

Throughout the years several attempts were made to reconnect, the most famous in Irish lore being Brendan the Navigator. After Saer's departure from Noah, Noah was instructed by the Lord to prepare for the return of his adopted son's family, though it would be years hence. Noah formed a select group of learned men to prepare, the Ashkenz. These men were resolute and learned, willing to wait for the union.

They formed small communities, created self-governing rules and clear religious rites.

Both families hoped for an eventual reconnection for neither knew for certain if the other had been able to succeed through the years. Worse, the Society could not be certain that their strategy of playing advisor roles only, never power positions, was being practiced by the family of Noah. Who was in power? Where they part of the rise of Islam? They had to discover what and where they could reconnect. They joined expeditions through the years, as well as continued to infiltrate different peoples and kingdoms.

James Jr. asked his father, incredulously, "So, you're telling me that a few men from an island at the far end of the known world directed the events that shape our world?"

"No, of course not" James Sr. laughed. "Listen, these men of the Society were few but intelligent and connected. They paid attention to those men seeking the financial backing of their kings for their journeys. They listened to the plans and safety precautions, learned their histories and past successes and failures. While no journey then was guaranteed to be fruitful, those with the greatest chance were often found to have a member of the Society on board. For example, a member was part of Marco Polo's trip and he was the first to make a connection in the Orient."

The James' looked at each other, father appreciating the doubt in his son that he himself had. This was his boy. He knew he should continue the story.

"Now, my boy, these trips allowed the Society to eventually reconnect to the family of Noah, but almost too late.

The history of the Ashkenz reflects a nomadic spirit, a wandering spirit. Without contact for centuries, the Ashkenz began to wander and in the middle ages, they were clearly located in France. But, the elders only sent those people out without deep knowledge of the mission. They were to establish connections and gain local knowledge. This was then to be sent back to the elders. However, more often than not, these travelers settled, became part of their communities, and let their objectives slip. While they settled and prospered, they became known as Ashkenazim.

This failure to return news unsettled the elders, and after much discourse, it was decided that one large excursion must be made, including the sagacious elders. When they had set out, one descendent of Noah stayed behind in Alexandria. For hundreds of years he and his family prepared and waited for the return, for the connection to be made. Finally, around the middle of the Crusades, Alexandria was becoming too dangerous for a man with children. One last expedition was sent out, in hopes of connecting with the descendants of Saer. The message was simple: come to Cairo and seek out a man with the names Wahed and Stella, "one star". He is the connection to Noah's family. The Society had received the previous message, but expeditions to reconnect either failed, or were untenable due to war or other conditions. This last message again was received and raised some alarm. Why was the Noah family abandoning Alexandria? But, dealing with the Norman invasions at home, it was again shelved. Finally, in the late 1700's, as the West was focusing on rebellion and revolution, the Society was able to discreetly reconnect with Wahed Stella in Cairo.

Emotionally, it was two lost brothers meeting for the first time. Logistically, it was a mess. For various historical, cultural and social reasons, the family of Noah had remained local, only in the regions of Israel, Lebanon and Egypt. Furthermore, though the Society had agents throughout the Middle East, there had not been a connection made. For Noah's heirs, their knowledge and connection was deep and secure, but they were small. The Society was larger and more complex, and had already made some agents in the Middle East. It took several years to mesh both organizations and keep everyone satisfied. The Noah clan maintained control of the Middle East; the Society realized the benefit of the position and work. Meanwhile, the Society was understood to be the umbrella of both, directing the ultimate mission. It has been seamless for over 200 years in its operation.

Cairo, with over 16 million people, is an easy city in which to disappear and blend. The Society and its agents have a firm foothold and use the city as the stepping stone south and east. The mineral deposits, the oil and the human capital are an untapped resource waiting to be opened by the Society.

===

Chapter Twenty-nine: The Present

As with any successful organization, planning was essential. As Western Academia became more thorough and scientific, so, too, did the Society. Each member was still seen as intelligent and capable, but there was a realization that the time was fast approaching when single entities might no longer suffice for the mission. Through the centuries the Society had expanded from Europe and northern Africa to Asia, the Americas and Oceania. It was a truly worldwide network, requiring world class and sophisticated guidelines.

So it was that in the middle of the nineteenth century, there was a great restructuring. There were two years of suggestions, a council of 20 selected, and a further two years of writing and analyzing.

The new structure was based partly on history, experience and the improved science of organization. Some basic changes were minimum age for new recruits (Jean-Luc's actions still echoed in the Society memory) and a mandatory retirement age from "active" work. The language and culture of the Society were reinforced through more regular regional meetings. A limit of twenty members per country was instituted, with no more than five to be approached within two years.

The new system cemented regional members' unity and thereby strengthened the Society. Communication, difficult for anyone during the expansion of the sixteenth, seventeenth and eighteenth centuries, was made easier through the more cohesive organization. With better information, better decisions and better "advice" were proffered by the members in their countries. This dissemination of information was essential for the successful approach to new recruits. Recent struggles for the Society were the infiltrations of three world powers: the United States of America, China and Japan.

Early on, the young United States were identified as a potential power. After the War of 1812, it was clear the nation would survive. However, with the independent spirit of their ancestors, and the renewed distrust of European powers, infiltrating the decision makers was an intricate process. It took years before any Society member reached any true level of influence. Even then, the government itself proved to be paradoxical, with its intelligence agencies investigating potential plots against the government; in essence, seeking out the Society. More often than not, it was a rogue agent – probably with that independent American spirit of the wild west – who snooped into the threat of outside influence on the government.

Years before the world caught on, and especially after the Sino-Russian war of 1908, China was identified as a "must have" sphere of influence. When Marco Polo departed, and one member remained, the Society felt confident they would expand. However, here, as in the rise of Islam, the physical characteristics almost doomed them from the start. A Caucasian face in an Oriental crowd was noticed, and often distrusted. The actions of the British navy as China opened up for trade did not necessarily aid, either. Several were tortured or killed, some were expelled. Nonetheless, the population, the depth of history, and the appreciation of the natural in

China all worked to create a favorable atmosphere for the Society. If the Society was to achieve its eternal mission and work for the salvation of the world, this country must be opened. Especially after the rise of Communism, the Society fought vigorously to maintain successful members. The first successful entry into China after the Polo expedition was made with an expatriate, encountered while on board a ship leaving China. An expelled member discussed his plight with a young woman fleeing her family for Britain. She was abandoning her home because she rejected the role she was expected to play in life, and thus was rejecting her entire past. The Society member seized the moment and almost instantly converted her to Christianity. Eight years later, she returned to her home, committed to preparing her family and her countrymen.

Japan had one major obstacle preventing successful placement of a member: the Emperor was the god of the people. Any talk otherwise was blasphemy and punishable by death. The fear of the people was not mortal, but for their eternal souls. Even listening to blasphemous talk scared them, and so they quickly betrayed the identity of the members. Finally, after the defeat of Japan in World War II, the people were susceptible. Their god had been beaten. Maybe, therefore, he was not a god? That was the opening necessary, and five recruits were quick to join.

Through every action, those in history books and those omitted, the Society began to affect the direction of mankind. Whether under the name of Christianity, Judaism, Islam or Taoism, the members worked for the mission. And the mission was soon to be realized. The entrances into China and Japan in the twentieth century were lynchpins in the success. Oddly, however, while the end of World War II allowed for Japan to enter the fold, it created a host of problems. By placing Israel in the Middle East, the British created one of the most belligerent confrontations in history between Jews and Arabs, especially Arab Muslims. Had the Society been new, it would most certainly have failed. With its history and dedication as guides, however, the Society was able to sidestep much of the distrust.

The Society currently finds itself, like most of the world, in a new global dynamic. Although immune from the oscillations of politics, the changing landscape of war and terrorism posed new challenges.

===

Chapter Thirty: Details of the Meeting
East of the *Gaeltacht*, Co. Donegal, Ireland

Clearly, the Society had thrived through the centuries because they were careful, learned from their mistakes and were dedicated to the ultimate mission. The original design, 2000 years old, was still basically in place. Wars, famine, revolts, demented leaders and paranoid kings had been unable to dislodge the Society. Each year, they progressed. Converts to Christianity had increased every year worldwide.

A mounting threat to the society started in the first years of the 20th Century. With the rise of super-powers, access to the ultimate decision makers became more difficult. Worse, a new wrinkle in humanity was the increase of atheistic leaders and nations where the mere mention of a faith could send a person to permanent, and guarded, exile. Their strategy and tact were at the ultimate test. As with the entrance into the Islamic world, it took several years and many failed attempts. However, by changing their vocabulary, their approach, and their methods, they were able to grab the ears of the leaders. Remaining there often meant overlooking atrocities, and several were tempted to quit rather than watch brutality. The discipline and the mission of the Society were strong enough, though, that these men were able to focus on the long term goals.

Furthermore, these new super-powers had their own secret initiatives and covert operations. In particular, the United States, Great Britain and the Soviet Union elevated their efforts to international proportions. While their existence was almost disclosed several times, the Society had avoided detection. This ability to remain hidden from the best intelligence agencies led to a general disdain for the CIA and MI5. As the meeting was being planned, this was not overlooked.

James Jr. had gathered some of the more senior members to help him plan the meeting. In the midst of discussing the secrecy of the meeting, he made a snide comment about meeting in the MI5 headquarters and still going unknown.

James Sr. grimaced. He had personally been involved during the Great War in helping the Society avoid detection, and he knew how much MI5 had in their files. One or two snippets of information would make clear to them the Society. Furthermore, he knew the CIA had a dedicated group to the discovery of the Society. While many in both offices saw it as a waste of time, there were a dedicated few who were convinced they would not only discover the society, but that said discovery would benefit the world.

He was not the only one to grimace. Vladimir Stolichnakov also grimaced. He was on the other side of the War and was also well aware of how much information was actually known. He and James Sr. spent many hours in counter intelligence and misinformation in order to protect the Society.

Looking at each other, they knew they had to warn the others not to be rash and foolish.

"Son, you should dismiss that which you know not."

James Jr. looked up.

"Listen to your father, son." said Stolichnakov.

"It is when you underestimate your enemy that he surprises you. He is always listening, watching and waiting. We are not the only ones engaged in such activities."

==

The details for the meeting were triple checked, and the security precautions tightened.

This was to be the last meeting, the send-off for the most progressive action of the Society in its history since Saer explained all to Conor. They would reveal the mission of the Society to the world.

The meeting was to take place in Malin Head, Donegal. It would last but a few hours. Each country would send their most experienced envoy with an aide. Members who had previously only spoken by phone or through paper would have this opportunity to look into the eyes of their comrades, their partners.

Avoiding detection upon arrival and departure was of the utmost importance. The numbers of visitors had to be balanced and measured, and the avoidance of patterns of arrival or departure was urgent. On paper, such paranoia seemed comical, with costumes, fake accents, travel re-routing, and even "missed" connections all part of the plan. It was like a bad spy movie. But it had to be done with every detail planned, every contingency understood, and even the possibility of a re-scheduled meeting realized.

==

In the past, it was physical power which persuaded men to obey leaders. Visible weapons, fresh blood and echoing shrieks were the tools of domination. Recent history changed that. Now, it was the threat of attack which persuaded men to obey.

With weapons thousands of miles away and beyond sight, with invisible viruses capable of being disseminated through the air, men feared the threat of power. Along with that came symbols. With the immediate physical threat gone, power was transformed into a national symbol, either a building, a monument, a religious site or even a man. This was the method the Society would use to bring the message to the people.

And so the Society was taking this bold step. On the surface, it seemed counter to its ancient strategy of being the power behind the throne, or merely influencing people to come to the message. That had been in accordance with Free Will, albeit on a human level. This action was stretching the concept.

The meeting's main purpose was to set the final date for the worldwide revolution. On that day, each chapter of the Society in every country of the world would stage a *coup d'etat* and assume political power of the country. Each chapter had identified the key symbol for their people and for years had been planning on its takeover. Bloodshed was to be avoided as well as possible.

Stolichnakov grasped James Jr. by the shoulder. With a firm grip, he said, "It is all necessary. More important, it is all worth it. Our lives are for the mission greater than us, greater than this meeting, greater than any plans we may have. Worry not, my young comrade. Worry not, only be committed."

"Be committed." repeated James. "Aren't we all committed to the cause?"

===

Chapter Thirty-one: Watching JT
Santiago, Chile

Gerardo's men were watching JT literally almost every second of every day. It was made crystal clear that failure to catch any possible weakness would bring dire consequences for the man, and for his family.

The work was oddly difficult. This American did nothing out of what was expected. He went to school, work, the café, home and back. He had a small circle of friends, spent some time with the Chilean host family and went on several business trips. The boredom of their jobs alternately allowed for mental lapses or jarred them to be hyper-aware of the ordinary.

The only flaw in their surveillance was they were late in beginning. Once on JT, they watched all his interactions and investigated every person with whom he came in contact, even if it seemed happenstance. Hence, each cabbie was checked; the clerk at the Post Office was cleared, and even some of the microbus entertainers were investigated. Every single check came up clear.

It all came up clear because their surveillance was initiated a day late. Mariela was approached the day before surveillance by José Luis, and convinced. He knew she would be watched soon, and he knew he had to communicate with her without showing his face. The setup was simple enough: the cardboard sleeves used by the café on paper cups would be "ordered" by a front company of José Luis's. An agent dressed as a delivery man would then re-deliver the case to the café. Mariela simply had to check the middle column of sleeves in the box for the one designated for JT. She pocketed it, waited for JT, and slipped it on without anyone noticing. On the inside of each was a message for JT.

That first day, when Mariela flirted and told him to keep the sleeve, was the opening salvo to JT. When he arrived home that night and put it on his nightstand, he noticed the writing. The instructions were so simple it scared him, and the reality of why some precautions were necessary scared him even more. He would receive messages this way. If he had something to report, he was to take the sleeve into a bathroom stall and write it then. His room and office were probably bugged, possibly with video. By using bathrooms in random locales – the university, a sandwich shop – he could avoid being seen to write. By returning to the café and flirting with Mariela, he could have her "trash" the sleeve while providing him a new one.

If only Gerardo's men started a day early, they would have seen José Luis talking to the café girl and, as a precaution, investigated both of them. But they did not, and could not know what they missed.
==

José Luis knew what they missed. Gerardo and his men had been under surveillance for years. They probably knew they were watched to some extent, and surveillance was possibly reciprocal, but it still helped. He was certain they were not present when he approached the girl, and so there was no way they would notice the method of communication. If JT followed the plan correctly, it should be safe.

Ignacio and Pato also watched JT. Initially, they were hesitant to use their home as a covert site. It would mean their home, their phones, their parents would all be monitored, by several different agencies from several different continents. Even with being in the espionage business, this was a disconcerting thought. However, they knew of both MacNessa and the little general. They knew that what happened in the seventies was not simply a coup, or a madman acting alone. They knew the American CIA helped the little general, and that he, in turn, helped expand their interests there. His actions almost severed his ties to MacNessa and the heads of power in Chile, in spite of ostensible gain for them.

Their knowledge of MacNessa was as limited as that of Pete Blood's. After S. Timothy's return to Chile, he was instructed to update an attaché in the Chilean intelligence. That happened to be Señor Cotarín. As his sons progressed into their father's line of work, he informed them of this aspect of his job and the importance of it. If this MacNessa were a real group, and the little general was both part of, and independent of, the group, they must know it to protect their Chile.

Over the years, snippets of information, unknown words, sudden disappearances and reappearances of the little general and some of the major powers in Chile, all formed a hodgepodge collage of a group working towards a global movement.

"But for what?" asked Pato, as he and Ignacio walked through the park. "Even as we work, I am not certain I know for what we are working!"

"I know, I know. At times, I doubt as well. What is the "Coming" mentioned by the dying Auggie? Did the American agent hear him correctly? The Coming sounds religious, yet the little General's actions have been anything but religious. Was he splintering off? And if so, why does he still seem to act beholden to another?"

"What if he tried to break away, and was, in whatever their goal is, unsuccessful? Would he be accepted back? Could they trust him? And to do what?"

Both brothers were very frustrated.

===

Chapter Thirty-two: The Semester Ends
Aconcagua de los Andes, Argentina

As the semester was winding down, JT and his host family were on great terms. Once or twice they even took him along with them on family vacations. Though he felt like an intruder at first, he soon came to realize he was experiencing Chile like few other international students could, or would.

They stopped at tourist spots designed for Chileans, not for foreigners, and therefore more special to JT. He was able to see the Río Bio Bio in the lower Andes. He danced to "Me gusta baila baila" in Los Ángelos with a friend of the family. Already enjoying the Chilean alcohol *pisco*, he was introduced to *chicha* while learning a Chilean card game.

This time away with the family allowed him time to reflect on his recent choices. It had been a complicated semester. This trip, these new experiences helped him see that making choices enriched his life. He was able to see that most of the choices were most vexing in the moments preceding the decision. Once it was made, moving forward was natural and therefore not headache inducing. Trips with the family, which seemed awkward at first and which he almost politely declined, proved to offer him insights into the Chilean spirit; insights which can not be read in a guide book. Not everything had turned out as he would have planned – his time away led Janey into the arms of another – but the value of taking the risk time and again surfaced.

Just a couple weeks before semester end, a couple guys from the school wanted to go camping in the Argentinean side of the Andes. JT was invited and readily accepted. All semester he had been working diligently in school and for both Gerardo and José Luis. This was a chance for him to unwind, and, in a way, to repay some of the kindness of the Cotarín. He invited Pato and Ignacio.

Pato was away that weekend, but Ignacio was available, and accepted. JT, Greg, Jerry and Ignacio packed up and headed out on a Friday at noon. Fortunately, all were friendly and the conversation jumped back and forth between sports, wine, business and politics. As Jerry, Greg and Ignacio were debating, JT stepped out of the conversation. Here were three people he met over 2000 miles from home and without whom he could not imagine his last six months. The beginning had been difficult; finding new friends and learning the living arrangement of another family had frustrated him several times. He felt stupid, alone, strange, awkward and nervous for close to a month. Now, he was calm and engaged with every person he met. School, the family, his friends, his time with José Luis and Gerardo all served to foster his maturation. Yet, he would be leaving shortly to go to Egypt and, basically, re-do it all. He would have to find new friends, and he would have new classes. Worse, at least with Chile he knew the language. He had no idea what Arabic sounded like beyond an Eddie Murphy comedy tape.

The weekend camping was great and their location was incredible. They found a mountain lake in sight with the peak Aconcagua and set up on the shore. They hiked, they went exploring, they stayed up late drinking and talking, they roasted marshmallows and fought the freezing cold night air, and they huddled together in the tent as random animals milled about their tent in the wee hours of the morning. JT was savoring the time.

Possibly JT's immediate favorite moment was the lake dive. Somehow transported back to being thirteen years old, they challenged each other to swim across the lake. Each dipped a toe in the water; chilly would be the understatement of the millenium. Nonetheless, each felt they could do it. Each was incorrect. Instantaneously upon their skin touching the water as they moved forward, they tried to move backward and undo their dive. JT's lungs froze and his gasp never left his throat. Thrashing about like caught fish, no one made it past ten feet. The water was so cold that not one felt the scratches on the bottom of their feet from the sharp stones. Numbness hit faster than a bullet.

Laughing and screaming and freezing, all cares were gone. That night, as they sat around the campfire, JT realized this was a great time for him. Jerry, Greg and he would each be studying elsewhere next semester; Jerry was returning to study in Colorado, and Greg to DC.

"What if we stayed here?" blurted JT.

"What?" said Greg. "In Chile?"

Ignacio perked up. He knew what intelligence next semester in Egypt could provide. What was JT doing?

"Think about it. How great a time are we having? We all know the routine, we know the city and we know the schools. Let's get an apartment, call our deans and stay one more semester. Imagine what we could do if we were living in an apartment downtown. We could set up our own network and be able to travel back every year; hell, Greg, you already have an internship. We could go camping, and go out to bars, and watch soccer."

"That does sound tempting. I could probably arrange it. You, Greg?"

"I could probably do it, too. And it would be fun. And to think about it, when will we get this chance again?"

"Exactly" echoed JT. "Let's say at lunch Monday we figure it out."

Ignacio cooled. This was a spur-of-the-moment thought by a young man enjoying his friends. Once they returned to the city, it would be forgotten.

==

"How was the weekend, JT?" asked Gerardo as he walked into the office.

"It was great. The Andes are incredible. Cold, but incredible. Actually, would it be okay if I left a little early today? I'm meeting the guys to share pictures."

"Of course. But we have a meeting at 2 pm which will last until 4 pm, and I need you there. *¿Está bien?*"

JT went through the rest of the day and walked into the meeting unaware of what the subject was. That is to say, he did not know he was the subject.

In the meeting were Gerardo and Octavio Ramón de Mojica.

"Um, *buenas tardes, señores. ¿Cómo están Uds.?*"

"We are well, young man, *gracias*. Thank you for coming. Please have a seat." replied Octavio.

"Remember those meetings I mentioned, how you were to soon be working and not simply mingling? This is the first." followed-up Gerardo.

Octavio began quickly to describe his goals for JT's role in the coming months. There was to be an international corporate meeting in the coming months, and part of the preparation required interaction with Egypt. Given the content, Octavio was personally thanking JT for continuing his work with the Santiago and Philadelphia Chamber of Commerce. This will greatly aid in their communication.

"You see, JT, our business interests are beginning to become more tightly bound to some industries in the Middle East. As of now, we have very few people we can trust, and we need people who know the terrain. If you are already there studying, you will become quite familiar with the details of daily life; how to take public transit, how to deal with cab drivers, what the local customs are. If we can talk to you directly we can help eliminate misinformation. Does this make sense?"

"Of course. But, will this affect my study time?"

"JT, when we found out you would be willing to continue your good work with us, we checked out Egypt. No doubt your dean reviewed your plans with you?"

"Oh, yes, he did. I realize I have plenty of time off. But I was hoping to travel then. So, my other time will be in class, and if it is limited to begin as a result of holidays, I'd like to focus."

"What if I said to you that not only will the work allow you to study, but, during your time off for the Eid holidays, we will help finance some of your travel? Would that be something of interest to you?"

Octavio explained that several industries were trying to form a merger. Due to the complex nature of the work involved, and the political entities who would undoubtedly take interest, they needed JT. In a tone which was instructive without being condescending, Octavio and Gerardo alternated describing international, high stakes business.

"It's sad to say, but it can be like one of your American mafia movies. People are killed, papers are burned, secrets are betrayed. Great amounts of money change men's morals. On our end, we have spent decades wheedling out corruption and incompetence, and we seek high achievers. We know you have the aptitude to become a contributing member. As we said to you, this first semester you have performed well. As a result, we trust you for next semester. Think about how your life will change, how we can help you, if you perform just as well in this capacity. Can you feel your brain working now?"

JT could feel his brain working. If José Luis was even half-correct, JT was being tested for possible future imparting of high level knowledge. His ramblings over the weekend of staying were in no way about to happen. He could not stay in Chile.

"High level? Secret? Mafia like? Excuse me, Gerardo, but I don't want to die. When you told me this job would open opportunities, you never mentioned I would have to risk my life. How crazy is this?"

Octavio and Gerardo smiled.

"Listen, JT," said Gerardo, "you are in no risk. Part of the benefit of your working with us in this role is that no one knows about it except Octavio and myself. On the record, your employment with us will terminate when you depart. For any prying eyes who may notice you worked for us here in Chile, they will never suspect that after a mere half a year you have been assigned such high level work. The chance that anyone would even notice the connection is slim. Think about it, put it in perspective. No one will know but the three of us in this room. Think about it, and we'll meet again this Friday."

==

After JT left, Gerardo's *tío* entered from a side room.

"It is, as you said, *increíble*. This young man is perfect. Move forward and have him transport the necessary paperwork to Cairo. Make sure he remains unaware of the full weight of the papers. Arrange the meeting with him. Choose an out of the way location; should be easy in that desert. Everything needs to be in place as quickly as possible. There can be no mistakes, not now."

"What about JT? Do we keep him under surveillance?"

"For what?" answered Gerardo's uncle. "Nothing has arisen. I am as cautious as the next, but we have spent weeks watching and investigating and this man is as you say he is: a college student happy to be studying in another country. You see, gentlemen, if you trust in the mission, God will provide little miracles."

All three men smiled as Octavio passed around glasses of wine.

==

JT walked into the courtyard and saw an empty table. As he sat down, he let out a breath. This was notching up the intensity. His breath froze again as he saw two figures approach.

"JT, how are you? I'd like you to meet a friend of ours. He is cover. For this to work, you must be seen with two friends, no?"

JT smiled. Everything seemed so simple, and yet...

"How did you pull this off?"

"Simple. We saw Jerry drop film off last night. We broke in, made duplicates and left the originals. Then, we left messages from you that you could not meet for lunch and you would call them. Just make sure you do so from a pay phone. Here, palm through these and smile as we talk.

Listen, JT, the semester is ending. Before we plan for your next year, do you have any updates?"

"Just one, I guess. Gerardo said something in passing about a flight to Shannon in May."

So it was Ireland.

"Well done, JT. Anything else?"

"As for intelligence? No, that's it. But, I did want to talk to you about next semester. I'm not sure I want to go. They talked to me today about what I may be doing, and it sounds like my life is at risk. I did not sign up for that, for you or for them. I had a great time this weekend, and staying in Chile sounds like a great plan."

"JT, you are free to do as you please. And to

be blunt, you do have reason to worry. This is not a game. But do not make your choice out of fear. Do not make your choice based on what you think might happen. Make your choice on what you know, and what you know will come to pass if you choose not to study in Egypt next semester. And I don't simply mean our work; what will Gerardo do? Are you close enough to scare him? Will he tolerate some random American with a good quantity of knowledge of his organization running wild, either in his own country's capital, or that of the United States? This decision is not so easy, and is not so clear cut."

JT hesitated, and put the pictures down. "What would you do?"

José Luis had not made it this far in this business by being unprepared. He knew this question was coming and given his previous take on JT, he knew this was a delicate balancing act. Worse, he kept placing himself in JT's position. Would he himself go? Would he run? Would he return to the safety of the USA?

"Pick up the pictures, JT. Someone might still be watching you and your friends."

===

Chapter Thirty-three: Gerardo Bids JT Farewell
Aeropuerto de Santiago, Santiago, Chile

Gerardo had one last meeting with JT. After work one day he bought him a glass of wine and a cigar at a local tavern. He handed over a list of coded names and numbers. JT was to make contact after one week.

"Gerardo, I can't thank you enough. This job has been incredible for me. I've been able to travel and meet people I never even knew existed. I have learned about business, politics, even life."

Gerardo smiled. He liked this young man.

"JT, why do you think I do what I do? Why do you think I work so hard? My work is not simply tasks and duties. It is not corporate work for monetary profit. My work is my mission. I live, breath, eat and drink it."

"I know how hard you work, Gerardo. It has been something I used to motivate myself in moments of lethargy in the office."

"Good, that is good. Use that in the coming months. You are a little nervous; your work is important but frightening. But realize what you are doing. Carrying these contracts will help us better the world. We are not simply looking to merge companies, but peoples. We do not want our own lives to improve but the lives of our countrymen. If – when – we succeed, you will have been an integral part of the success of us all. Know that I appreciate your work; Señor Ramón de Mojica appreciates your work. And when it all is official and we are moving forward, we will thank you again. *Vaya con Díos*,

JT."

They shook hands and parted. JT was shocked; Gerardo basically confirmed everything José Luis had ever said. It was true, it was all true. Gerardo was using him as a pawn in a game. Was he actually carrying contracts? He desperately wanted to look, but knew he was under observation.

"Hi JT." chirped José Luis. "Buy you a drink?"

"What the…" interjected JT. "Where, how, what are you doing?"

"Come here, let me buy a you beer."

"But, what about…"

"Don't worry. Your surveillance was removed over a week ago. At least by Gerardo. We never cease ours. He's gone, in his car and on the road. Whatever you said or did worked, he has no fear of you. And he has no knowledge of our communication."

José Luis also provided JT a list of names and numbers as contacts in Egypt. The contact over there would initiate communication. JT was to learn the streets and neighborhoods as quickly as possible. On the flight, his passenger seating assignment had been arranged to allow for an Arabic tutor to sit next to him. He would be provided a book and some CD's. When he left the flight, all materials were to remain with the tutor. No one was to know he was beginning his language studies.

"What good will that do? The flight is a total of twenty hours. I'm not going to learn a language in that period of time."

"Now, now, JT. Have you not learned to trust

me by now? We have methods which accelerate language acquisition. You may not be fluent when you de-board, but you will be able to understand and read Arabic much faster if you follow our tips. This in turn will advance your ability to function well in Cairo without making a commotion. You will be able to move seamlessly. The less attention, the better."

"What if there is trouble? What will happen?"

"Perceptive question." answered José Luis. If he could tell him the truth, he would. "Do not worry. As we have men here, we have men there. You will be provided. We have protected you here and your safety is a primary concern. And once our work is completed, your life will return to normal."

Whatever that means ran through both their minds.

===

Chapter Thirty-four: Tears

When JT first saw the pictures of Janey and another guy, he was crushed and immediately okay'd working for José Luis. But as the days wore on, he could not forget the girl he loved so well, so quickly. Even though Mariela was pretty and fun, Janey kept haunting his memory. The fact that she kept sending him letters only increased his pain. He finally had to compose one last letter... to end it.

Dear Janey,

The past few weeks have been difficult. Work and school have been testing me. Not having you near me pains me, and I can't say not having you here by my side tomorrow will be any easier. But, if I can't see you tomorrow, if another guys gets to hold your hand and kiss your lips, if another guy gets to make you laugh and hold you tight, it's best that we stop writing.

I don't know what I am going to do; Chile has been fun and Egypt lies before me. The choices to be made are difficult, as is this one, but the time to decide is now. You and I must move on.

When I will see you again is difficult to say. If I can, later, I will write. For now, let's say that we were important to each other, and realize that the choices we make in life often change our plans for us.

I'll never forget you,
JT

JT read the letter. He could only tell her so much. And it was true that he would never forget her. He could not, however, pretend the pictures did not exist. It was not a friend in that picture; it was a new guy. His hand on her back. His lips on hers. She had not waited. He signed it, sealed it in an envelope and walked to the post office.

It was not until he dropped the letter in the mail slot that he started to cry.

===

Chapter Thirty-five: Answers Demanded
Washington, DC

When Janey received the letter, she re-read it a dozen times. What was he saying? Was he ending it? Was he not coming home between Chile and Egypt? Did he find another girl?

Recent calls to the house went unanswered. Until this letter arrived, Janey merely thought JT was busy, or maybe starting to enjoy himself, something he needed. But this letter scared her. She loved JT, wanted to be with him. Letting him go was so difficult that only love allowed her the strength.

The last few letters had been awkward, as if JT was afraid to be honest. Then there was that two week span where Janey did not receive one letter at all. Not even a postcard. She started to phone Dean Bulgiuno, concerned that JT was having problems. Each time, the Dean did not accept the call.

Dean Bulgiuno's secretary came to know Janey's voice. It was heartbreaking to hear Janey plead for information, to explain that she loved JT and only wanted to know he was okay.

"Even if I cannot talk to him, please tell me he is okay and appreciating his time in Chile. Please."

The secretary finally broke.

"Listen, Janey, the Dean will never tell you anything. He feels it is his duty to be stoic and, in his mind, protect the students. But here is the name and address of the doctor who spoke to JT. He might be able to help you understand."

Instantly, Janey phoned Dr. Ogilvie's office. There, she also received the runaround. Frustrated and angry, Janey left a message that she was showing up one day at 9 am and was not leaving until she spoke to him, even if she had to sleep in her tent outside his office door.

==

"Ah, damnit."

Grelsh listened to the voice mail and could tell by the tone she was serious. She was going to sit there until she was arrested or told something. A big problem with being Dr. Ogilvie was the lack of an office. A PO Box covered letters easily enough, but visitors would not meet in the Post Office. If she came to the address provided by the secretary of the Dean, she would find herself in an abandoned apartment complex. He had to call her and meet her somewhere. And he had to think of what to tell her, what she would believe.

==

Adams Morgan was as good a place as any in DC to meet, in a nice bohemian coffee shop. Grelsh arrived a half hour early to scope out the place, and Janey was already there. Damnit, he thought.

Janey was sipping her coffee. She had no idea what this Dr. Ogilvie looked like, but she figured they would need a table and some privacy, so she found a corner nook and waited. Anxious, she had asked a friend to come with her. Stephanie was over at the counter reading a magazine. Janey kept eyeing each single male who walked through the door.

They made eye contact and each knew.

"Janey, a pleasure to meet you."

"Dr. Ogilvie, thanks for meeting me. I'm just so nervous and no one is giving me answers and I'm worried and…"

"Calm down, dear, calm down. Have a seat. Let me get a cup of coffee and we'll chat. Do you need a refill? A muffin?"

"No, thank you, doctor."

She was intense, no doubting that. And captivating; as he ordered coffee, Grelsh could see why JT – and the hapless TJ – had fallen for her. This was going to be challenging.

"So, can you explain what's happening? The Dean's secretary said you might be able to help."

"Well, Janey, I can. But, in order for me to do this, you need to trust me. I am here because I like JT and I'd like to help him as he moves forward. Realize that I am the only one who will talk to you, but if you won't believe what I say, I might as well leave now."

After agreeing, Grelsh started to weave his tale. He spoke to JT once a week, sent letters once a month. JT was having a tough time in the beginning, mostly because he missed her.

Janey suppressed a winced smile.

"And so, I had decided to come over and talk to you on campus, to let you know some things you could do to help him more fully appreciate his time in Chile yet know he was coming home to his girlfriend. That was a couple weeks ago and when I was walking over, I saw you walking with another guy. I would have written it off as just friends, but the way he was constantly touching you, my thoughts wandered. And as he leaned in for a kiss, I turned away."

"No wait!" screamed Janey. "You don't understand. We're just friends, we're not even friends.

He was trying to hit on me but I pushed him away. You saw that, right?"

"Well, like I said, when I saw him lean in, I turned away. I knew JT would be devastated, and I could not watch knowing I would be unable to keep this from JT. Oddly, as I walked home, the thought struck that it might serve JT. If he knew you had moved on, he would be forced to face his own situation."

"But, but it's not true" Janey repeated, urgently grasping Dr. Ogilvie's arm. "None of it is! What gives you the right to judge what I'm doing without talking to me?" she demanded.

"Nothing gives me the right. I saw what I saw. My concern was JT. I did not even know you. I was not, and do not, judge. I know separation can be difficult and if that was how you were dealing, that is fine."

"I was not dealing!"

"Nonetheless, I felt I had to tell JT. As an advisor, as his advisor, I had to help him. He was crushed. We were on the phone for hours trying to grasp what had happened. I called him a couple days later to touch base and he was still upset. But, he knew he was not ready to accept. That's why some of the letters in the last few weeks were, well, less than enthusiastic. Finally, a week ago when we spoke, he said he was ready to move on. His classes were engaging him, his friends were fun and adventurous, and his host family was warm and friendly. So, we discussed it. He could not handle hearing your voice. The distance would have made the situation unbearable and writing a letter seemed to be the best method to communicate. He read me the letter, and I thought it…, well, I knew. There was a lot of pain in there, but also a great deal of strength in moving forward."

"Well, call him, tell him it's not true. I'll bring that guy you saw to your office, he'll tell you I turned him down. JT needs to… , what? Why do you have that look on your face?"

"There's something else" said Grelsh in a lowered tone. This was tricky. And for Grelsh, meeting this girl and knowing that, had he not interfered, the two of them would still be side by side, it was a tense moment. He felt the personal responsibility of his actions.

"Well? What else?" continued Janey.

"Just about a week ago, JT told me he went on a date. He had found a girl who was interested in him. They had been flirting in a café for weeks, and finally, they went out. They had a great time. He was already planning the next couple of times out with her."

Janey gripped the table as a life preserver. Completely unprepared for this, she could not even cry.

"Janey, this is only because he thinks you moved on and he should do so, as well. It has nothing to do with a loss of feeling for you."

Janey looked up, with hope in her eyes.

"You're the doctor. How much happier would he be if he knew I still want to be with him and am waiting. Let's call him."

The plea ate at Grelsh.

"I am the doctor, you are correct. And, as such, I disagree. I don't feel telling him will help."

"What?! What are you saying?"

"Listen, JT has had a trying past couple of years. His life has been in almost constant upheaval. Even this study abroad, which I feel will ultimately benefit him, is an upheaval. You were a rock and helped stabilize him, but, maybe he needed to figure some things out on his own. Maybe he needed to be cast adrift in order to learn to swim. Part of the trip that is therapeutic is the distance from his past life."

Grelsh touched Janey's hand.

"All his past life."

Janey's head dropped a little.

"And?"

"Janey, lift your head. Look at me. You love JT, and deep down, you know he loves you. You could read between the lines. It's why you are here. Now, he is on his own, living, studying and working. He has to figure out what he is doing. *He* has to decide. When he comes home, the two of you can work out whatever situation needs resolving. If you love him, let him finish this semester on his own. When he returns, face to face, your discussion will be much more effective than over a phone line 3000 miles long. Make sense?"

Janey nodded.

"Go home, relax, spend some time with your friends. You enjoy your semester, too. This is a time for you to rejuvenate. If anything arises, send me a letter. My schedule in the next few months will be hectic; I have to do a great deal of traveling. My secretary will open my mail. I'll leave instructions to contact me if you write. Let's get through this together, huh?"

Janey nodded again, but was softly heaving with sobs. Stephanie came over.

"I should get going. He'll be okay; you'll be okay" said Dr. Ogilvie, and he walked out.

Was it Grelsh or Ogilvie who felt it? Either way, one of them or both did not have the heart to tell Janey that JT would be traveling to Egypt, and not DC, after the semester.

===

Chapter Thirty-six: Egypt Awaits

"The Pharoah approaches!" shouted the watchman. Standing at the base of the palace, he was to greet the pharaoh and bathe his feet. This new pharaoh was legendary already for his strength, his wit, and his ability to woo ladies.

"Right, to woo ladies" snickered the guard. "What lady would turn down the pharaoh? Actually, what man would turn down the pharaoh? To do so means death. Let's hope his strength and wit are real enough."

He bowed as the pharaoh approached.

"You highness, welcome to your new palace. Please follow me."

The pharaoh was led to the throne room, already overflowing with well-wishers and connivers trying to appeal to his good graces.

"My lords and ladies, honored guests, it is my honor and privilege to introduce to you the new Pharaoh sent to us by the gods as a blessing to our future, the Pharaoh JT!"

Screams and shouts of joy were complemented by applause and foot stomps. The pharaoh smiled and waved his hand. The gifts were being brought for inspection: gold statues, fresh fruit on diamond covered platters, wild animals tamed for his amusement, slaves captured in war and, last and most appealing, the women available for marriage. These were brought in one by one, wearing jewelry and perfume, little more than leaves as clothing, and silver sandals on their feet. Each did a little dance, thanked the pharaoh for the honor of his sight, and kissed his feet.

"My Lord," whispered his servant, "of course, you may spend a night with those whom you feel might suit you. Select one now, and she shall be waiting for you."

The pharaoh smiled. He gazed out the window, past the throng of people and saw the sun setting over the wondrous pyramids, almost highlighting the gaze of the sphinx and reflecting off the ripples of the Nile.

As the party continued, he walked down the marbled hall to his bed chamber doors, covered in rubies and emeralds. Beyond the door was the selection for the night. This one had eyes dark and deep, flowing brown hair and soft, ample curves. Her legs had shimmered as she walked, the oil reflecting the candle lights. He was captivated instantly, and since it was his royal duty to appreciate such beauty, well, he would indulge. After all, he was pharaoh.

He opened the doors and beheld her, standing next to the bed, wearing even less – an impossible feat in his mind – than when he saw her just moments ago.

"My king, my noble warrior," she said, "is this seat taken?"

The pharaoh JT squinted his eyes. What?

"Excuse me, is this seat taken?"

JT woke to a large, mustached man in a brown suit asking to sit next to him on the flight. No beautiful, almost naked woman? No marble floor? No fresh fruit on trays?

"Um, no, make yourself comfortable."

"*Shukran*." said the man.

"Excuse me?"

"Shukran. Thank you. I appreciate your kindness. I am Wahed Stella." He offered his hand.

"I'm JT. Nice to meet you."

JT was one of the first to board. The entire time he was waiting he felt a pull to open the package Gerardo had given him. What was it? Would it be worthwhile to know? Was it really a contract? Or was it something worse? Sure, he might be watched by José Luis's men, but José Luis said Gerardo's men had ceased their surveillance. And weren't he and José Luis on the same team?

No. This is not a game. His life was at stake. Everything during the semester had gone well, everything; to commit an error like this now would be beyond foolish. He was trying to think of Egypt when this man interrupted his thoughts. As it came rushing back to him, he grimaced.

"Idiot!" JT mumbled to himself.

"Pardon?" said Wahed.

"Oh, nothing. I just realized I left my book in the airport lounge."

"Ah, well. Tell me, do you go to Egypt for leisure or labor?"

"Oh, I'm going to study for a semester."

"Fabulous, a student. Are you always open to study, then?"

JT looked at the man, and then at his bag. Language books. A CD player. He had almost forgotten.

"Absolutely, I'm always open to learn."

===

Chapter Thirty-seven: … it is a shame.
Santiago, Chile

"It is a shame. He is such a bright young man. He is dedicated. If we had more time, we could welcome him in to the fold. But, well… it is a shame."

"*Sí*" concurred Gerardo. "*¡Qué lástima!*"

"Well, so we move forward. The question is how."

Gerardo smiled at his own efficiency. When JT left the house of the host family, Los Cotarín, he ordered the surveillance team to make one last sweep. Just in case. Nothing of consequence was discovered, and all their bugs were able to be removed to prevent detection. However, a small envelope was discovered. It had come from the girl in the United States. They knew about her, of course, but the last few weeks she had fallen off the radar. It was a typical study abroad situation, and since everything else with JT had proven safe, they dismissed her.

But this letter was an opening. In it, the girl was bemoaning their lack of communication, and pleaded with JT – knowing he was feeling the pain also – to write to her, to talk to her, to come back home. It was obvious that JT had broken the news that he was ending it. The pain in the ink was palpable, and the moment Gerardo read it, he knew JT had a weak spot to be used.

"In Egypt, how we will end his relationship with us?"

"Unfortunately, Octavio, we must end more than his working relationship with us. He knows our faces, he knows the people with whom we communicate, he knows where we are. We must end more than his relationship. We must erase it so none may see."

Octavio looked. Gerardo was correct, of course, but he was continually amazed at how he thought more and more like his uncle.

"So, ¿cómo?"

Gerardo explained the letter, mentioned the surveillance of his flirting with the coffee shop girl.

"So?" asked Octavio.

"If he was flirting after such a painful breakup, he is open to meeting a new girl. But, he will be susceptible to suggestion. This letter is our key to get in his head. All we have to do is have one of our associates sidle up to him. Make him feel loved, needed. We have an associate over there, one from an older family. She will know how to handle the young man when the time comes. Heck, she might even enjoy the ride."

"Keep going."

Gerardo explained about Alicia. She was from the first Norman family to be approached by MacNessa after their invasion of Ireland. With roots in England, they began to set a foothold there, as well. She knew the mission and was gifted in clandestine activities. She had not actually ever personally taken on such a task as this, but given her history and past dedication, it would be a small leap.

"But how will they meet?"

"Simple. I met JT on the rugby pitch. That worked well. I have a feeling JT will try to find some rugby over there. He knows he made some great contacts, aside from the recreational aspects of the game. We spoke before he left, and I encouraged him to continue the positive steps he took here in Chile. I did not mention rugby directly, but there is little doubt in my mind that it has crossed his mind. This Alicia plays rugby, I believe. We'll check. Nonetheless, we shall watch, and should he join a team, she will be playing for the girls' squad. There will be parties, they will meet. She will woo him there. If he chooses not to play rugby, well, she may bump into him and mention casually that she plays. It is simple enough, she is from an English/Irish background. In a foreign land where rugby is one of the few areas for English speakers to meet, why wouldn't she play? Besides, what else is there to do over there?"

Both men laughed, although a little uneasily.

This was not an enjoyable aspect of their work, no matter how many times they had to endure it.

===

Chapter Thirty-eight: NSA POA
Washington, DC

"Everything is set?" asked José Luis.

He was in Washington, now, talking to Grelsh. He was debriefing him personally on everything they had learned through JT. Now, they had to plan for Ireland, had to prepare for whatever might happen in Egypt, and they had to broaden the scope of MacNessa.

"Yes, everything is set. We have a marine over at the US Embassy in Cairo. He is about the same age and also plays rugby. Clearly, part of this is a gamble. We can't guarantee that he will continue to play. But we know one of his future roommates played with him in college. Beyond that, we know that part of a new tradition over there is for the US Embassy to host a Super Bowl party into the wee morning hours to watch the game live. Mostly they get the American college students. That's the second angle. We'll continue to look and plan for other openings, but if one of these works, our marine will run with it."

"And then?"

"And then. And then, and then..." Grelsh trailed off. He walked over and poured two whiskeys. Sitting down he let out a long, slow sigh. He turned towards the window to face the city before him. José Luis felt the same.

He walked over and stood next to Grelsh, and looked at the same city. At least these two men were seeing the same things.

===

Chapter Thirty-nine: Roommates… and Agents?
Cairo International Airport, Cairo, Egypt

Walking off the plane, JT was impressed with the language skills he was able to pick-up. By the end of the flight, he was looking over a newspaper and was able to identify all the letters in their various positional forms and to recognize many of the words. José Luis was correct, he was not fluent, but he was well on his way to acquiring Arabic.

JT had several guidebooks with him, and his friend Kimani had e-mailed him some landing instructions: don't get a taxi from inside the airport, walk to the taxi queue; don't let anyone carry his luggage; all the cabbies speak enough English to understand tourists, don't fall for a "monolingual" cabbie; and finally, don't pay more than 20 Egyptian pounds for the ride to the apartment complex.

Looking around the airport, JT was amazed. In the airport in Chile, he felt more in shock at being there than at the condition of the airport itself. Truth was that the airport was clean, well lit and maintained, and appeared like the airports he had seen in the States. This was not Santiago. The airport was dimly lit, the ground was dirty and sooty, and everything had the appearance of being frozen somewhere in the mid-1970's.

"What in the Sam Hill am I doing?" he thought to himself. "I am in freaking Egypt. Egypt! Are you insane?" He sat down and pulled himself together. Through the semester and via e-mail, he had discovered that several of his friends were also studying in Cairo. One of them had taken the time to mail him a map of the area where his apartment was. He took that out and read Latim's instructions. The student dorm was located just around the corner from the apartment complex, and any cabbie should know the student dorm for *Il Gema'a Amrikea*, the American University. Then, it was just a matter of going around the corner.

Pulling into Zamalek, his first thought was that living on an island in the Nile would make a great story for back home. His second thought was the result of looking at the area. Zamalek was – he was told – one of the wealthier foreigner residential areas. At this moment, it looked like a crowded urban jumble of buildings. JT was hoping the daylight would brighten things up.

He made it to his apartment and unloaded the baggage. He was exhausted. Trying to watch the new sights of Cairo just lulled him to sleep. Of course, the cabbie forgot his English when they arrived, and JT wound up paying close to 30 Egyptian pounds. He didn't care. He just wanted a nap.

He arrived at the floor and knocked on the door, expecting his friend Kimani to answer. Nothing. Knock again. Nothing. Panic crept into his head: he was in Egypt without knowing the language, without having a map, at night when the university offices and, therefore, the study abroad office, was closed. Even as a last case, he knew no one from either connections with Gerardo or José Luis. No contact was made. Was he lost? Where would he go? Who could he call?

"I don't even know how to use the phone here!" his panicked mind screamed.

Just then the door opened.

"Oh, hey, you must be JT. Come on in. Nice to meet you."

And so JT met Charles. Charles was a journalism and Arabic language student from Quebec, Canada. There would be four of them in the apartment this semester, but the other two were out traveling. They would be back in a few days. Actually, most students were traveling. This was one of the Eids JT had been told occurred frequently in the Spring semester.

Did JT want to grab a cup of tea with Charles and his friend? No, he did not. JT wanted a nap. Where would his room be? Charles left and JT sat on the couch. He was in Egypt. He was in Cairo, in Zamalek.

He was tired, but he started to review his coming months. Everything was hitting him heavily. He had to work with Gerardo and José Luis. And, he still had to study. At least in Chile he spoke Spanish a little. His Arabic on the plane helped ease his transition, but even with his confidence in looking at one newspaper, he realized that twenty hours would not supplant years of classes.

"Okay, think. You have this work, that work, and school, all in a land where the language and alphabet you have never seen. What do you do?"

He eyed the map his friend Latim had sent him. Of course! He had friends here. Latim was here and so were Yoon and Neria, all friends from college. He would be fine. Right?

"Wait. What are they all doing here? Latim is Hindu and Indian. Yoon is Korean. Neria is Jewish and speaks French."

JT was pacing now. Where they in on something, too? Was the NSA approaching his work with various students, various angles? Did José Luis send them over the semester previous? What about Dr. Ogilvie? Was he in on it?

Everything was scattered in his mind. He walked into the bathroom and splashed water on his face. Looking in the mirror, he laughed. He had to calm down. If they were in on it – whatever "it" was – then they had their own problems. He would make contact in a week with Gerardo's men, and then, soon after, José Luis's men would contact him.

"Just use your head" JT said to the mirror. His friends were his friends. He was tired, dirty and ready for a nap. He let out a soft chuckle. His whole life was nowhere close to where he thought it would be. The Dean and the Doc had diverted the course of his life. Were they doing so for the right reasons? What about José Luis? How honest was he? Was Gerardo what José Luis said? Could his friends in Egypt be his contacts? Looking at himself in the mirror, he squinted. All he could do was accustom himself to Cairo and the American University. He had to.

"You have to be able to trust somebody."

===

Chapter Forty: After One Week

JT had a great first week. Kimani and the other roommate, Brian, returned from travel. He made calls and spent time with Latim, Neria and Yoon. All of them were excited he had decided to travel to Egypt and they dove into showing him around. Neria even took him to an Italian restaurant, in case the Egyptian food did not sit well with him. Combined with the activities of the study abroad office, JT was very busy. He learned about *shisha* cafés and tea, about backgammon, about the rules of the student dorm and about the network of ex-patriots all over Cairo.

The ex-pats were one of the greatest resources for entertainment and connections. The ex-pat bar was Deals, located just a half mile from the apartment. JT spent a couple nights there and met a few Brits, some Irish, a couple Aussies and New Zealanders, even a few South Africans. He was having such a good time, he almost let the week pass without making contact.

Around dinner he realized he could not simply go out again. He picked up the phone and made contact. The man who answered called himself "Isman". He wanted to meet at 9 p.m. at a shisha shop. JT cancelled his plans for the night with his friends and waited.

At 8:45 he went downstairs and hailed a cab. He gave the name of the café and sat back.

"You like shisha, my American friend?" asked the cabbie.

"Um, not sure yet. This will be my second time."

"Oh, trust me, they are very good. You should

sit back, inhale the smoke, sip some tea, and recall your days in Chile fondly."

JT sat up. What the…? Was this "Isman"?

The cabbie laughed. "Do not worry, my friend. I am Isman. I am here to help. You have something for me, yes?"

JT handed over the package, still unopened, as Isman verified.

"Very good. Now, let me tell you how to make contact in the future. The telephone will not do."

There was a little internet café near the apartment. JT was to go there and set up an anonymous internet account via Hotmail. The user name was to be "arturopratt@hotmail.com". He could send messages only to "victorjara@hotmail.com". He was to check in at least once a week, regardless of whether or not he had any work to report. Anything suspicious was to be reported. Local customs and habits would be helpful and he was to forward his schedule once he was settled.

"Any questions?"

"Just one. Um, now that we met. What I am supposed to do tonight?"

Isman laughed and pulled into a shisha shop.

"We smoke and drink. My treat. Come, let me show you Cairo."

The two sat there and chatted. Nothing too personal was shared, but JT felt comfortable learning about Cairo while smoking and drinking tea. Maybe the work would be easier here. And maybe Isman was just a good guy. Maybe.

===

Chapter Forty-one: The Wooden Ring
The Wooden Ring

James Sr. and James Jr. were busy preparing for the meeting. Each had details for their contacts to plan and alternatives to create. It was tense work, but each immersed themselves into the work.

James Sr. had seen the network grow and increase its power and influence. Possibly, it was at its greatest strength in its history. He was passing his life's efforts on to his son. Still, he agonized over it. He loved his son. He was intelligent, dedicated, funny and warm. Had he chosen any another path, he would have found the same success he saw here. As he doubted when he told the family history, he doubted now.

There had been some bumps in the road over the years. Latin America was always a challenge, as was Asia. Both eventually were brought back into the fold; the Society was very efficient. Should his son lead the society through the coming bumps?

Looking out his office window, he knew he had to share with him. He slowly walked over to Jr.'s office and sat down.

"Son, I need to tell you something."

James stopped writing and focused on his father.

"Sure, what's on your mind?"

"Do you remember the story of Ferceirtne and his daughter? How he waited the appropriate amount of time to inform her of the calling?"

"Of course. He was watched by the others, as well, to ensure his objective continuance of the mission. Why?"

"Well, son, it is time for me to reveal another step to you. You know that we are the keepers of the wooden ring." he said, raising his right hand. "And you know that I am getting older. It is time for me, for us, to consider passing the ring."

"Oh, father. Let's not get ahead of ourselves. You are the rightful wearer. You are the head of our body, guiding us and channeling our energies."

"Relax, relax, son. I am not retiring. I am not stopping the Society."

James Sr. stopped and exhaled. Could he stop it, even if he wanted to do so? His own father did not even think about that possibility. He simply communicated the deepest secret to him, as had been communicated to him, as James Sr. would have to communicate to his son.

"Son, the Society needs a leader with energy, drive, intelligence and charisma. I have been fortunate to be esteemed as such. Everyone is looking at me, at you, as once they looked at Ferceirtne and his daughter. And you are ready. You are ready to take over the Society."

James Sr. coughed and held his chest. He stood up and poured a whiskey. James Jr. watched.

"Now is the time. As we transition the Society we must have a leader who will take the initiative. We have worked side by side for years. You have seen the inner workings. You know the key positions, key counselors and key strategies."

James Sr. coughed again. Sipped his whiskey.

"At the meeting, once it is convened, we will have a ceremony. In it, I will pass the ring to you.

You…". The father hesitated.

"You… you will be the bearer of the ring of Saer."

James Sr. clutched his chest, dropped the glass and fell to the floor. Jr. ran to him and pulled his cell phone out, calling the emergency services.

"Come on, dad. Hold on. Relax, breathe. There you go."

==

The doctor approached Jr. in the hallway and explained that the father had a small heart attack.

"A small heart attack? Is there such a thing?" asked James.

"Well, all heart attacks are large, sure, but this was able to be corrected quickly. Tell me, has your father been under unusual or extra stress lately?"

Jr. diverted the answers and then went to sit by his sleeping father's bedside.

===

Chapter Forty-two: After One Week and One Day

Both José Luis and Gerardo had been correct; JT did want to play rugby. Maybe it was the conversation at Deals, or living with an ex-teammate. Either way, JT had asked Kimani about playing, and he was on board. The guys at Deals had mentioned rugby, but never specifically where or when.

Kimani spoke Arabic and so was able to do some light research. Practices were Tuesday and Thursday nights out in an area called Maadi. The club was Cairo Rugby. They pulled into practice that first night and introduced themselves. Players came over and shook hands, welcoming them to the team.

Practice felt good, energizing. Kimani and JT were a little above the middle of the pack, not superstars, but solid. Considering most of the team was composed of Australians, Irish and British, they felt confident.

At the end of practice, as they were taking off their spikes, an American walked over.

"Hey guys, my name's Jason. I'm American, too. Good to know I'm not the only one out here."

They chit-chatted for a few seconds; JT and Kimani learned that Jason was a Marine stationed at the American Embassy near the University. After practice, the guys usually went for drinks and to shoot pool at their clubhouse. Kimani and JT were in.

"Good thing we brought clothes" chimed JT.

"Hey, can one of you new guys come over here" called the coach several yards away at the bleachers.

"I got it" said Kimani, and walked over.

Jason and JT continued to pack up their bags, and change into casual wear.

"Hey, JT, listen, I'm your man."

"What?"

"I'm your man, here in Cairo. José Luis said you might play rugby. And he was right. We've been watching you all week. That cabbie last night, he your Gerardo contact?"

"Wow, you guys are good. Yes, he is."

"Good. Listen, you can probably get away coming to the Embassy a couple of times, if you need to tell me something. But, too often will raise suspicion. Like Chile, assume you are being watched all the time, by both sides. If Kimani is not coming to practice, we can probably get away with hopping in a cab together. So, the best way for us to communicate will be here at practice, never in a cab or any other closed environment. Twice a week regular communication is pretty good for a start. If we can't talk here, at least we can plan where and when. Sound good?"

"Uh, sure. But what if something pops up?"

"Well, we'll have to create some sort of contingency plan. Once you get settled and comfortable with your surroundings, we'll go over your days and seek opportunities. Anything else?"

"Not that I can think of now."

"Good. Now, how are you to contact Gerardo?"

JT told him quickly the internet e-mail addresses and the name of the internet café.

"That should be easy enough to trace. Well done, JT. Well done."

Kimani walked over. Everyone was heading over to the clubhouse.

"What was that about with the coach?" asked JT.

"Oh, coach wanted to give us the signup sheets. Since we're students, we can pay less, but we still have to pay some team dues. But, we do get to go to the clubhouse and have some drinks!"

JT felt good after practice and surprised by Jason. These guys were good. Kimani felt energized. He enjoyed his time in the first semester, but he forgot how much fun rugby was. This would heighten his second semester experience. And Jason was enjoying the new assignment: play rugby, hang out at a clubhouse and talk to a contact. He could almost pretend he was with his buddies back home. The three of them packed up and hopped in a cab to the clubhouse.

JT could see Kimani and Jason and how comfortable they seemed, how the smiles on their faces appeared as genuine as he had ever seen. He let himself smile, and he let himself enjoy the comfort of the cab ride with his new friends...

===

Chapter Forty-three: From Legend to History
Grelsh's Office, Washington, DC, USA

José Luis was watching the skyline, comparing it to Santiago. Both had a beautiful mix of classical, colonial and modern designs. There were, however, stark differences in building style and in geography. One could place a shack in front of the Andes and the shack would look grand. DC, however, was the opposite; one could place the buildings in front of a trash heap and no one would notice the heap.

Grelsh sipped his whiskey and stood up.

Without looking, José Luis asked, "Are we doing the right thing?"

Both men had long ago seen the realities of life and believed in the mission of the Agency. On paper, it was noble and good. Clearly, off paper, there were abuses of power and resources. These men concerned themselves with their jobs, with their ability to further the mission for the immediate purposes of the country and for the long-term benefit, in turn, of all countries.

Grelsh did not answer the question. He simply poured himself another whiskey.

"Chris."

"You know, José Luis, for the first time in years, I'm wondering that."

"I think it's time you filled me in a little. Don't you?"

No time for bullshit, thought Grelsh. The actions they were taking and the risks with other men's lives would not permit that. Besides, it was he who invited José Luis up to DC after receiving that last package. And so Chris started to explain MacNessa.

He invited José Luis to sit down at a side table and pulled out a thick file.

"This file was started in 1913 by an agent named Brian Sullivan. He was a high level agent in international affairs. His parents were Irish immigrants, poor, from the countryside. They believed in all the old Irish legends and myths, from banshees and leprechauns to Blarney and faeries. Great storytellers, supposedly. Anyway, they regaled Sullivan all through his childhood with stories of the greatness of Ireland and its fabulous past, how peoples fought and died, how noble warriors and kings led a gilded age which was destroyed by the ravages of the English and greed of a few individuals. Being Catholic, the parents focused on the Irish monks and how, without them, the Catholic Church would have fallen into compete oblivion after the fall of Charlemagne.

This guy grows up and as a hobby researches Irish history and legend; becomes an expert on it. Around 1910 or so, this guy is frustrated with his job. Things are starting to heat up over in Europe, and most people back here are ignoring it, pretending that there is no influence to be felt. Long story short, he takes a leave of absence and travels to Ireland. 'Need to rejuvenate' was part of the reason given. This guy heads over there and reconnects with his family in the west of Ireland. He nose-dives into his family past, working the fields, singing in the pubs, everything you can imagine about being Irish. He even learns how to speak Irish. He was in deep. He may have melded into the countryside and never come out except for one thing."

"His research?" asked José Luis.

"Sort of, but not really. He was still researching, but it was less formal over there. Being in the midst of the culture he did not need books or libraries; he had story tellers and local historians. That started to affect him. It would be like a baseball historian being thrown into a clubhouse and beginning to believe the versions of stories only those ball players told. He was overwhelmed. What sparked his interest, re-kindled it maybe, was something he saw one afternoon walking home through the fields. He was going to wash up and have dinner when he glanced and saw a man walking near a cliff. Being friendly, he tried to hail him. Suddenly, the man was gone. Poof! Vanished! Sullivan raced over and looked below... nothing. No body, no traces of struggle or fall. The footsteps just vanished near some rocks on the edge.

The guy was freaked. He went home and stared at his fire all night, trying to figure out what the hell had happened. In the morning he went back to the spot and noticed there were more footprints. Nothing below the cliff, though. He talked to some locals, and asked if there were any stories about the cliffs. Of course, there were, plenty of stories of the hidden deDannan people walking the fields when no one was about, coming from the underworld to temporarily reclaim their land. No one gave it a second thought, except Sullivan. He knew it was a man, he was close enough to see his hair blow in the breeze. No spirit, no ghost would be affected by wind, right? He cracks out all his research and pores over the stories relating to cliffs. There were dozens of them. A couple had correlations with the monks and their ways to hide from Viking invaders. A couple of them deal with faerie forts, where the people had underground tunnels and as invaders came over the top, they snuck out and outflanked them. He hops on some freighter back to the states and got some equipment and then sailed back. Now, the equipment back then was crude, as you can imagine, but there was some rudimentary equipment to check for sonar and thermal pockets. He scoured that field, square foot by square foot. For the most part, nothing. Even near the cliff, he had a difficult time receiving a clear reading.

One day, frustrated, he sat down and rested. He was scanning the horizon, doubting himself and his equipment. Was it just the deDanaan people? Were the Irish legends correct and his technology wrong? Just then, he saw a man walking away from a large formation of rocks. It was half submerged, with grass patches all around. He jumped up and ran over. When he arrived, he saw three men on the side, chatting and smoking. They eyed him suspiciously. What was he doing in Seamus' field?, the tall one wanted to know. Sullivan was smart enough to defray his thoughts and introduced himself as a neighbor. The men prevented him from getting too close to the rock formation. An untrained civilian would never have even noticed what the men were doing. They were good, but Sullivan was better. They were defending something. The look in their eyes and the tone indicated they were not amateurs, and they would not hesitate to use extreme caution to defend whatever it was. Sullivan would need to be prudent in his approach.

He took his time, surveilled the landscape, got

to know his 'neighbor' and slowly formulated a plan to uncover the meaning of the rocks. He found some places he could hide and eavesdrop; he listened and watched. From time to time, he found himself privy to some snippet of a conversation, or he found a small piece of paper or rock with mysterious markings. Several times, with his heart racing and feeling close to full disclosure, the neighbor or his wife would arrive and invite him in for tea."

"And?" asked José Luis. "This makes a great story, but what are you driving at?"

"Part of the reason this Sullivan guy was so adamant about all this was those snippets of information. He was experienced as an agent and knew the habits of other agents. He was learned, especially in things Irish. He heard words and stories which subtly enforced the idea that there was work being done by the cliffs. Some words he heard in Irish which were innocuous enough had a double meaning to natives, words in English like 'struggle', 'mission', 'rule' and 'power'. He watched random foreigners arrive and depart within a day. Nowadays, Ireland is full of tourists and business people. But back in 1910, there were no foreigners on the island. Everyone was either Irish, British or of Irish or British lineage. A dark skinned man, a man wearing robes or headdress, this was an oddity. The hushed arrivals and departures were even more suspicious, in spite of local lore that they came to see the cliffs and dream of Irish legends.

He knew he was onto something, but he also knew that if he was correct, there was no way he could handle it himself. He was back again on a boat to Washington and briefed his boss. His boss, his boss's boss, and his boss's boss's boss all dismissed it as Irish rebel talk, the IRA or IRB or whatever it was then, nothing more. Unless he could prove otherwise, he was to drop the issue and get back to work. By this time, it was 1913, and he opened this file. With permission, and by hinting that an Irish rebellion against England could affect commerce with the US, he was able to place a young agent in Galway. Nothing really ever built up; there was not too much to observe, not too much to report. But from time to time, an interesting arrival, or a sudden change in funds in a bank account, would find its way to Sullivan.

Most of the other agents dismissed the stories and the file as the fancies of an Irishman who heard too many stories. Sullivan finished his career anonymously. He was stable in his work, never too flashy. But he never forgot the file. Towards the end of his tenure, he encountered a young agent named Blood, Peter Blood. He was the son of Irish immigrants, and when he heard Sullivan telling Irish tales, well, he was hooked. Eventually, Sullivan filled Blood in on his file. Blood knew the rumors about Sullivan and his sanity, but as he read the file, he came to believe maybe everyone else was crazy to dismiss him so quickly.

After Sullivan retired, he moved back to Ireland. By then, he was too old to perform the physical feats necessary to follow up on his hunches. He and Blood maintained contact, but more than anything, Sullivan passed on rumors, sightings and innuendo. It came to a point that Blood began to doubt his own initial assessment of Sullivan and the file.

When I came into the Agency, Blood was getting ready to retire. But he felt some impulse, a duty... I don't know what. Call it sentimental attachment. Whatever it was, he selected me to inform about the file. There were one or two other agents who knew, but I was the one to whom it was fully revealed."

José Luis whistled as Grelsh took a sip.

"If the file is correct, Sullivan's work is of epic proportions. First, the details of what he thinks is being planned are catastrophic. Second, his work, then, is more important to pursue than anything else in the history of mankind. Third, if he was able to collect all of this information, pass it on to Blood and continue to collect, then his work was effectively done in secret and provides an incalculable edge."

Grelsh paused, and chuckled.

"Do you realize that part of the reason you are even involved in this is because a predecessor of yours gave concrete proof that MacNessa was more than an old man's fanasty?"

Grelsh filled José Luis in on S. Timothy and the final passing of Auggie. That information known only in Ireland would be mentioned by a dying agent in South America was surprising, if not alarming. That confirmation to Peter Blood had prompted the Agency to beef up the office down there.

"The CIA piggy-backed on our information and, as you are well aware, made some of their own moves in Chile. Auggie had been correct. But the actions taken by the CIA only confirmed to many that Auggie was merely discussing the 1973 *coup* instead of the larger MacNessa with which you and I are engaged."

Sipping his drink, Grelsh drank in the moment. This was the first time he was retelling the tale. He wanted to make sure he told it correctly, make sure José Luis understood the implications.

"If all the materials in the file come together as Sullivan thought they did, and knowing what we now know I think it does, then what you and I are part of, what the whole Agency will be soon part, is a full scale, worldwide attack on humanity, not some single country *coup d'etat*. MacNessa's ultimate goal is the overthrow of all governments, at one time, by a single group of elite individuals selected over time and through history."

"It's almost unbelievable" murmured José Luis.

"Ain't that the kicker? Maybe that's part of the genius of it. Who would ever suspect something like this? Most of the world is in upheaval, so one has to wonder if it just might work. If MacNessa has been around this long, has been planning for this much time and has a wealth of knowledge and resources as deep as its history, and nothing has yet been done, maybe they are waiting for the right moment? Maybe this is the right moment in time."

"Has there ever been an indication of when this would happen?"

"Nothing concrete, like everything else we have. What we can gather is that nothing will happen without one final meeting to ensure the details. This group is secretive and methodical. Once we started to trace financial activity and travel activity of suspected members in the late 1970's, we assumed a pattern would develop. It always has with any group. It may be complex, we may need mathematicians to explain algorithms or whatever, but one always appeared. With MacNessa, nothing. For some agents, that was enough to fuel their sarcasm and doubt. Mathematicians claimed there was no conceivable way for a group to continue operations without a pattern."

"So why did you stick with it? Why do you still believe this is working?"

"Maybe Blood passed on some of his sentimentality. Maybe the lack of a pattern was exactly what I expected as proof. I don't know. When I ran into JT, I was hoping against hope that nothing would happen, both with him and with his assignment. I thought maybe we can help this kid out, maybe he'll surprise us and prove to be a great agent down the line. He arrived on the scene at the right time. I never expected him to do any of what he did. How could I know that this young kid would be able to incorporate himself so adroitly into Gerardo's life? How could I know that Gerardo was essentially the contact to know in Chile, if not all of Latin America?"

"What do we do? What can we do without attracting attention or having the Agency shrink sent in to evaluate us? I mean, most of the people still think this is fiction, right?"

"All we know right now is that a large meeting is being planned in Ireland for May. We can't really go over and tell the Irish they have to dedicate resources and men, technology and money to a supposed international plot to overthrow the world which just happens to be centered in the West Coast of

Ireland."

"So..."

"So, we have to find our own resources, and we have to convince the Director that this meeting is more than a gathering of old friends or high society. Fortunately, with the state of world affairs, we do not have to sell the conspiracy theory, just that the meeting of such highly influential people being conducted in secret should be noted. We have a few days to prepare. We are working against time and we are working without a net."

"Who do we have over there?"

"We don't have anyone over there. Who worries about Ireland? As bad as planning has been with linguistic resources in the Middle East or Asia, it's even worse in areas where there was no recognized threat. We may have one guy over there we can contact, but there is no way we can trust him with the full purpose of his assignments. We'll have to find a couple guys, give them skeleton information. Then, once we have a date, we have to risk exposure and embarrassment. We need to make sure all offices are operational as we get closer to whatever that date is. No one will believe this is true until we have concrete proof of a meeting. Otherwise, you and I become the next agents lost in the Irish myths."

José Luis stood up and walked over to the bottle. He filled himself up and walked back to the window. He sipped and looked out. Grelsh walked over.

"This is a hell of a lot of information to believe, Chris."

Each took a sip.

"The implications for our actions will echo well beyond our lives, let alone our careers."

Grelsh nodded.

"I know. I know. I believe you."

José Luis looked at Grelsh and asked the next question with his eyes.

Grelsh cast his eyes downward. He looked out the window and back at José Luis. He could not give an answer with his eyes only.

"We both know our business. We have had to come to a level of acceptance of tough choices, sometimes painful, sometimes permanent. I like him, too, José Luis. I genuinely like him and would like nothing more than to buy him a drink when he returns from Egypt. But, if completing the mission successfully means I don't get to buy that drink, then, I have to focus first on completing the mission."

Both men cast their eyes down, unable to look out on the city before them.

===

Chapter Forty-four: Alicia
Maadi, Cairo

Alicia hesitated when asked to perform this service. Her family was already in deeply enough with the Society; hell, they had moved to Egypt full time when she was a child. There was no need, she felt, to expose herself to greater scrutiny and danger. On top of it all, she had just started a relationship with a British mid-shipman. Even if he did set out on assignment in a week, there was uncertainty. As for rugby, she had played some back in England. In Egypt she was not yet playing but she was not opposed to it.

When she showed up at practice, she was careful not to run right over to the men's practice. She did the drills and acquainted herself with the girls. A couple of weeks later, there was a game weekend, and the girls wanted to scrimmage the guys as a warm-up. JT was running scrum-half that weekend, and Alicia was doing the same. At the line-up, JT introduced himself. She was cute, he thought, and was glad he kept his mouth shut when the idea of a co-ed scrimmage arose. About five foot eight, Alicia had light brown, shoulder length hair. She was thin, but athletic, with light blue-grey eyes and soft, full lips.

The match was well played, and while the men won, the women knew they had held their own... and the men knew, too. During the game, JT and Alicia had a couple of chances to chat and flirt, and both had a good time. After the game, JT congratulated her and started to walk away. He liked her, but did not want to move too quickly. He remembered Mariela and realized that part of the reason he felt comfortable with her was because he got to know her over several weeks without any pressure. This girl was cute, and he was here for months, there was no need to hurry.

Alicia, however, had different plans. She wanted to meet this guy and determine if she wanted to invest herself in this project.

"You going to grab a beer? And if I buy," she started to ask with a slight mock flattering tone, "will you teach me to be a great scrum half?"

JT laughed. Of course he was going for a beer. And if she was buying, well, why not?

"My advice might make you worse" JT replied with a smile and nudge.

They chit-chatted and headed over to the clubhouse. Kimani and Jason made fun of him, but the night was – in terms of deeper meanings – calm. Everyone left happy and anticipating the next practice.
==

Alicia kissed her mid-shipman goodbye a week later. He was being deployed on a six month mission to the south of Africa. It was all the time Alicia needed. A message was sent to the Society. Alicia was going to sidle up to JT and work him.

===

Chapter Forty-five: The Society Prepares

James Jr. made the hospital his center of operations. Due to his father's position in the community, the hospital readily provided a "family room". Phones, a computer, small satellites and a fax machine were set up within hours.

James Sr. woke up at one point when no one was in his room and looked around. His son's jacket was over the chair, and he could hear activity through one of the doors. He knew it; his son was moving forward. But why? Was he doing it because of the mission? Or was it because Jr. thought it would be what he wanted? He buried his face in his hands to think.

"Hey pa, glad to see you up. How long you been awake now?"

"Oh, hello James. How are you? I've just now woken up. I see you've started…"

"Hold on there, pa. Relax. Breathe. Let's focus on you before we do anything else. How you feeling? You dizzy or queasy or anything? Feel weak or strong? You want something to eat?"

James looked at his son, his boy. "I'm fine, son. I could use a cup of coffee or something, but I'm not really hungry."

"With two creams and a sugar…" trailed off Jr. as walked out to get the coffee.

James took the moment to reflect. His own father had died of a heart attack years earlier. His was sudden and heavy and he was lucky to have a few hours of lucidity between the attack and his final breath. In those moments, as Jr. was doing now, he doted on his father. He loved his father. Everything they had done together for the Society had united them, made their paternal bond strong. But for James it was never the work that was his center. Sure, he was dedicated and trusted his efforts. But to be able to work side by side with his father, to be seen as an equal and to be respected by his father and his friends, that was the payoff for James. Maybe that was why the final moments with his father were not such a shock or blow to his life. Those final words coming from father to son affected not his view of his father. He knew work was work and people needed a purpose. That his family chose this, well, that was beyond him.

Within his reach was that style of father-son relationship; it was what he always worked to create with his own son. As he lay there in bed, in a hospital with his own heart attack, he pondered his own end. His father's final words took strength to utter, and courage and faith to say to his son. Did he have that courage? He had no way of knowing if this was his final ticket, so he scanned deep into himself. Had his father done the same mental review?

His thoughts were interrupted by Jr. bringing back coffee and danish.

"Alright, m'boy, now that I have some coffee, where are we?"

Jr. proceeded to explain the most recent preparations made. Basically, at this point, it was a matter of checking and double checking information, testing procedures and contingency plans, and steeling resolve.

Because it was so old, the Society's structure generally withstood the rise and fall of governments and their various regulatory agencies. It was easier to grandfather in an old company with documents and papers than re-write everything in new forms. Thus, many of the dummy companies used were never inspected or monitored. Furthermore, their intelligence system was a backup for them, allowing them to remain one step ahead of spying or interference. For years, the society had been setting up arms depots in various strategic worldwide pressure points. Logic dictated that for an economy to work, every single package, truck or cargo container could not be individually inspected. As containers came into port, most were shipped out unopened, especially when the inspectors noted the name of a reputable company which the Society held. Should one be inspected, the intelligence tip-off allowed for the company to alert the authorities that one of their containers had been hijacked. Some employees then played the part of hostages and some of hijackers. Time passed, the furor died down, the "hijackers" received parole. With this simple process, the Society held arms depots fully stocked and in secure locations.

"All weapons have been accounted for and all ammunition is cleaned, separated and ready to use. Trucks are gassed and ready to mobilize and all men are in position."

"And how will they talk to each other?"

Jr. laid out again the communications worldwide. They had piggy backed onto every major communications advance for the past 300 years. They had satellites in space no one knew about; they had undersea cables never noted on a map; and they had sabotage in place for all but theirs ready to go.

"When it blows, only we will have access to any sort of telecommunications. Every company, every pirate radio station, every country will be without the ability to reach their neighbor down the street. The shock will cause a sort of panic, but we estimate that the appearance of a face on TV's and computer screens – regardless of whose it is – will bring calm enough for us to move forward. The message will also be clear – we have the power."

"Good. Good. And how are we for finances?"

Finances had always been the tricky part for the Society but they learned from history. They watched as great names and kingdoms – the d'Medici, Spain, France, Timbuktu – all had eventually fallen under the weight of gold and its effects. Always seeking more, they exposed themselves to fraud, corruption, greed and outright thievery. The Society was not looking to get rich. They did, nevertheless, need money to finance operations.

"Has there been any compromise in the integrity of the books?" asked James Sr.

"There have been a few pricks, a few close calls, but nothing with substance and no one who has continued to probe. It is safe."

Money was generally kept as liquid as possible, with gold bars the preferred method. Diamond mines in Africa, silver and copper mines in South America, and stacks of cash in banks worldwide added layers of comfort.

As for banking, the Society was there at the birth of the Swiss Banking Industry and knew its ins and outs. Numbered accounts kept billions of dollars safe. The recent inquiries into Holocaust accounts had nothing to do with them, but the probe was the greatest threat yet to their Swiss activity. Patience won out, nothing was moved, and, consequently, no suspicion was raised. The hundreds of corporations around the globe made for easy transfer of money for purchase of vague goods and services.

In the Industrial Age of England, a wise member realized a gaping weak point was individual wealth. As traditional monied families had to contend with "upstart" *nouveau riche*, the acquisition of money was questioned. While ever a consideration since the days of even Conor's society, personal wealth was quickly tempered within the Society and strictly accounted for in each country of each member. The Society moved quickly to mollify the differences in attitudes and reaffirm their singular purpose.

"Amazing, pa, every dollar, deutschemark, drachma, franc, pound, peso and now Euro, has matured and earned interest in the safety of the organization."

"With a well run organization, with good men and women, and with the right intentions in their efforts, should it be any other way?"

As father and son discussed the details, each continued to savor the moment. This was just the two of them, rehashing what had been discussed innumerable times. The information was known like their names, but by focusing on the information itself, they lost themselves in the moment as father and son. The next statement was as much from the leader of the Society as it was father to son.

"There will be retaliation and revolt. Are we ready to cope with that?"

Retaliation had been the greatest concern of the Society for years. With each new member into the fold, the message had been enough. No one had ever been forced to join. This next step, this evolution of the Society, was changing that. While they were not directly looking to convert all peoples into believers, there was a certain expectation that the message conveyed on such a scale would win the world over easily. The MacNessa family had always endorsed such a reaction among the members. No doubt, no hesitation was ever evident in the demeanor of a MacNessa to indicate otherwise. In private, however, words changed.

"We have exhausted ourselves in simulated responses, from passive to active, from passive aggressive to guerrilla warfare, from terrorism to sabotage. Everything that has ever been done, everything that has ever been dreamt up, everything that any nut-job author described in a book has been tested and re-tested for the past 20 years. With each advance in technology, our simulations have shown more effective resistance. So, too, however, has our effort been more capable in its response. We are ready.

"There is no cause for concern then?"

"Well, father, in every case save one, we have seen complete victory within three years. Those are incredible odds in our favor."

"And what was the one case which thwarted our efforts?"

"On a whim some years back, I was joking with Seamus about how we were so successful in our efforts. Youthful pride, I guess. Anyway, we realized our strategy, misunderstood by outsiders and thus never applied well, was patient and quiet. Seamus joked that it would be a hoot if some other agency used our strategy against us. We plugged it into the simulation. With this strategy applied against us, we still see victory in three years."

"Good, as long as victory is assured…"

"Well," Jr. interrupted, "the immediate victory is assured. With every other simulation, complete control was established within 15 years. Any resistance at that point would be similar to the efficacy of the independence movement in modern Puerto Rico. They are considered fringe and their position untenable. However, a resistance to us using this strategy has a slight possibility for successful overthrow within ten years. In twenty years, it has a fifty-fifty shot. In thirty years, it has close to a 90% chance of success."

James Sr. was lost in thought, his brow furrowed and his head now pounding.

"You alright, da?" Jr. asked.

"I'm fine. I'm fine. It's the threat over time which weighs on me."

"And me, too. Don't forget, I'm a front man here. True enough, there is much to plan, but would we have done this work if we had no faith? There is always a risk for failure, in everything. The planning, the time – literally thousands of years – and energy in the Society has prepared us. Come on, da, have a little faith in your boy! We have run every simulation. We know there will be some members lost; everyone is prepared. But, ultimately, we know that before 10 years can pass, hell, before 5 years can pass, the message will be out and there will be no need to defend a revolt."

"No need?" asked the father.

"Of course we realize that it will take time to win over several billion people. That's simple logistics. And the biggest struggle will be the beginning. Nonetheless, every indicator we have, in spite of the one simulation, has shown that our message, our objectives and our ultimate structure will win over all who hear. Pragmatically, we have learned our lesson from the Christian proselytizers in the Americas and Africa, from the Muslim preachers in Africa and southern Europe. Our techniques are finely tuned and honed and will reduce people's impulse to reject change. By alleviating fear, and maintaining a visible status quo, people will wait. And there will be no retaliation once people hear and see the Society and the work it has conducted for the good of mankind."

"I know, son, I know. Everything done is for the good..." James Sr. sipped his coffee and looked down, "of humanity."

Jr. smiled and walked back into the other room, not seeing the tear drop from his father's face.

===

Chapter Forty-six: Grelsh Prepares
Washington, DC

Grelsh was fortunate to be on good terms with his boss, Director John Maloney. He knew that John did not buy into the Sullivan file, but he also knew that John hated terrorism and fear as tools of war. Being Irish, John also held a special place for ending the sectarian violence in Ireland. He did not care who started what – Catholic or Protestant, Irish or English – he just wanted the bombings and attacks to stop.

That's where Grelsh found his opening to get some agents and some funding. Information on Ireland's activities was never scarce, and generally, was limited to the island, *per se*. With a little clever piecing together of information and a convincing sell job, he was able to convince John that both the IRA and the Ulster Volunteer Force (UVF) were looking to expand operations among supporters in the United States. To counter it, Grelsh needed some men on the ground in Ireland and in the US. That was the easy part. Men and women could be shuffled around. Funding and equipment, that was the kicker. Grelsh had to convince John, who eventually would have to convince a Senate Sub-Committee, that spending ten to twenty million dollars was worthwhile. And why running submarines around the world on "training ops" was worthwhile.

"Explain to me why this much money is needed again." said John.

"One word: propaganda. What we have always been taught is to look to history. The biggest successes, and even some failures sold as successes, have been received as such because the people believed the propaganda. Hitler rose to power with great propaganda. We need to be able to counter any propaganda the IRA or UVF put out, both here and in Ireland. That means we need people reading and writing, preparing pieces for newspapers and internet blogs. We need people who know how to use the internet effectively, who know how cable and satellite information are transmitted and how to directly target those to whom the information is most important. This will tie in statistical analysis and market research. With better equipment and manpower, the more rapidly and effectively we can do all this."

"Okay, I'll bite. Why the worldwide military involvement if Ireland is generally confined to the island?"

Grelsh here had to use a little history, highlighting the Irish diaspora and how the "Wild Geese" of the 1800's had planted seeds of Ireland worldwide. The men and women who fled English persecution did not forget from whence they came; they did not create brand new songs to erase the old ones; they did not write new histories or stories to shield their children. Pubs in New Zealand and Australia, South Africa and Argentina still had regulars who could belt out "The Irish Rover" on a whim.

"If they are fanning out, then they are ramping up. They already have training grounds in the Middle East, and one can only imagine the pockets of arms depots around the world into which they dive after every new truce is signed. I'm not saying we'll need the subs, but given that most of them are non-coms right now, wouldn't a training op serve them? And a training op in key positions may be in our own best interest."

Grelsh stood there, watching John ponder the argument. What he was doing – lying to get federal funding, misleading the military, misappropriating funds, and doing all of it on a monumental scale – would not only cost him his job and his career, but could also cost him his freedom. The US government generally, and the US military specifically, do not take kindly to being lied to by a man on a personal mission.

John weighed the information. It was a bit of a stretch, but given the state of world affairs, precaution was the best path. Grelsh had always been one of his most reliable and productive agents. He had no reason to doubt him now. He approved the finances and the manpower and, most importantly in Grelsh's mind, the submarines. Everything would be set for the meeting date.

Immediately, Grelsh set to work selecting agents and positioning his communication network. Sub-groups were formed and each leader had essentially a co-leader in the communications point man. He set up a network, new from the ground up, in ten key cities, with the focus being on Europe, Asia and North America. The sophistication of the new technology allowed them to test and communicate beyond the normal scope of frequency in use. Constant self-monitoring and change kept the agents sharp.

He contacted the commanders of the ten submarines he was maneuvering for the op and explained his timeline and his thoughts on what they may need to do. As much as possible, they were aligned around the globe on two paths, almost like a ladder. They were free to come up with their own cover in case of detection by another country's military.

He flew to Switzerland and reviewed the funding. The US had also been around when the Swiss Banking Industry began and had its own series of financial arrangements. Grelsh made sure the money was there and available. He also made sure he had reserves for any necessary side deals to accumulate intel or to gain access to whatever may be pertinent to his work.

Grelsh and José Luis were in almost daily contact. Gerardo was monitored constantly, like most suspected members of the Society. Both men barely slept or ate, but neither lost energy. They knew this work, they embraced this work. They were wholly dedicated to stopping whatever it was upon which Sullivan had stumbled close to one hundred years ago.

While both realized if they were wrong, it was Grelsh who would feel the heat, they also realized if they were correct there would be enough heat to spread around. Neither man liked to lose in anything; both were willing to make an exception.

===

Chapter Forty-seven: Alicia's Loyalty
Cairo, Egypt

When Alicia and her family first came to Cairo, she was a little hesitant about the move to North Africa. She was happy in Ireland and England, going back and forth between her family estates. Sure, she had taken classes which involved information on Egypt and Africa, but she had never delved into the politics, the people or the language. But, like most things in her life, she charged forward and began to take classes, attend lectures, and acquired a private tutor to learn Arabic. Quickly, she came to realize that, for the region and the information she was digesting, Hebrew was necessary. Fortunately, her British passport allowed for easy travel back and forth to Israel. Wherever she went, she engaged people in discussions on the state of politics in the Middle East, its root causes and possible resolutions.

Fact was, most people did not want to deal with others. And with each passing discussion, her faith in the Society and the work of her family deepened. Clearly, this was a region begging for external control and order; it would never be achieved through traditional peace talks.

After she met JT, she continued the same practice of engaging in discussion and debate. JT had been doing similar things. His work with both José Luis and Gerardo had been slow of late. He mostly dropped off packages and, since most of the packages were delivered with a specific time frame, he had no chance to open and inspect most of them. Plus, he found that by engaging locals in discussion about their lives, they were more open to talk, invite him over for tea or meals and meet him out socially.

As they first started to broach difficult topics, both took the time to feel out the other's positions and arguments. What JT had, however, was the benefit of time and distance. Alicia had been living in Cairo for some time and had not had the chance to go back to visit either Ireland or England. JT, meanwhile, had been home and then thrown into Chile. All the while, he was constantly conscious of his own life and why he was doing what he was doing.

The "discussions" often turned very heated and both would raise their voices. There was no anger, but the debates were lively and detailed. Often, they would argue for hours before realizing it was past midnight, or one of them had missed an appointment. In the beginning, it would be fair to say neither budged in their positions. Issues were dissected, words were parsed and semantics were exposed, but neither moved.

"So your basic position is that order is preferable to individual liberty. Is that what you're saying? You would rather live under an imposed rule from outside than set your own?"

"What I am saying is that for some people, consciously or not, that is the preferred method of life. Everyone cannot be king or president, everyone can't have the same amount of money. There have to be differences. And unless we understand that, we'll continue in the situation of today. Look at the Middle East. Everyone wants to be ruler of their own country, they want their neighbors ousted and all are willing to fight forever. If order were imposed, if education was consistently applied to both sides, eventually, over time, the people would come to understand the benefit of following set rules."

JT smiled because he knew this was his opening. The first point was small, but clear. The second would close the first major gap in Alicia's logic.

"First, tell me how many people you know who want to be king, or president? Not just in daydreams and fairy tales, but genuinely want to be in that kind of a position with all the accoutrements of responsibility and pressure. Most people I know, most people with whom I speak, want to be left alone to live as they see fit, to worship as they see fit, and to enjoy themselves as they see fit. Of course, you might need to consider the level of people with whom you speak. No offense, but if you have estates in three countries, odds are you are not dealing with average income and average education individuals. Ask yourself how often you actually have had conversations with people who earn less in a year than you do in month. From where you are, you speak to a limited circle of people. Their perception of daily life and what real work is remains vastly different from the average citizen in any country. While their points are valid, their numbers are small and therefore not representative of the majority.

Secondly, and more importantly, let's deal with order imposed from outside to quell differences. You're presuming that human nature is taken out of it. People who are different will always know they are different. Order is not having to love your neighbor, it's celebrating the differences and loving your neighbor because of them. Furthermore, what if the chaos you describe was itself imposed? How will order and education imposed on peoples eradicate the differences already imposed? You tell me, how well has your Ireland responded to the "order and education" imposed by the English? Has imposition strengthened or weakened the disdain for the other's differences?"

That was it. They talked for hours and they continued to go back and forth. Time and again while discussing their current geographic locale of the Middle East, JT brought up the decline of the English Empire and, specifically, Ireland and England. Alicia's ancestors had been Normans, imposing their order on the Irish natives. Then, as the Norman English stayed in power, they tried everything in their power to control the Irish. Nothing was working.

Maybe there was a flaw in the logic. Maybe imposition was not the answer. With that, JT unknowingly had Alicia begin to question her loyalty to the Society.

===

Chapter Forty-eight: Gerardo's Trip
Santiago to Cairo

Gerardo pulled out of the airport parking lot smiling; he genuinely liked JT and was glad he was able to be there to send him off. But it was time for business. He knew he was watched at the airport, and he also knew that with JT gone, the surveillance would slack for a bit. He picked up his car phone and called his uncle.

"*Sí, se fue. ¿Y yo? Yo me voy.* I'll be on the last flight out tonight. I'll bring you something nice, eh?"

He hung up the phone and headed home. He pulled in, took his bag out of the trunk and hopped on the next micro to the office. As he moved up in his career over time, one of the advantages of not having his car at work was the ability to use one of the secret exit tunnels. Many a clandestine meeting he had attended, returned to the office, and exited the front door to be surveilled again.

This use of the tunnel was not a meeting only. He had to get out, hop a military jet and make a connection in Buenos Aires to Cairo. And he had to be back in two days. Beyond that, sleeping at the office became too suspicious.

Everything for the trip went smoothly and he pulled into Cairo to an awaiting cab.

"*Hola*, Gerardo. *¿Cómo estás?*"

"*As salaam a lekim*, Isman. I am well, *shukran*. How are you?"

The two men chatted as Isman wove a path to Alicia's place.

"Are we going to make her do this?" asked Isman.

Gerardo smiled. He knew Alicia's father and family for years, and knew they were as dedicated to the cause as their forefathers had been to invading Ireland. And Gerardo knew that any doubts she might have would be disarmed by JT. It was amazing how JT warmed up to people so quickly. They would not, of course, force her to do anything; coercion had historically delivered poor results. Worst case scenario, they brought in another agent. Gerardo, however, was confident she would acquiesce. He needed to prepare. He needed to prepare before Alicia met JT and before whatever surveillance the Americans set up would detect her.

The cab pulled up out front and was met by a mini-van. Three men jumped out, nodded at Gerardo and Isman, took out a double drain sink, and all went inside. They walked right into the kitchen. The set-up was simple enough, really. The new, double sink, was actually a method of communication. The second sink pipe was a functional sink. With a flip of a switch, however, the pipe opened into a separate pipe which sent the messages through a whole separate piping system.

The system was brilliant, and the only problem ever really encountered was how to install the pipe so it was not obviously new, and how to ensure the agent knew which way to flip the switch for the correct purpose! In this case, Alicia's sink pipes went right through the floor and into a basement filled with pipes. By placing the new pipes behind the old ones, they had camouflage and were able to extend the piping into the street access sewer and connect it to their system.   To the naked eye especially, but even to a trained eye, it looked like another pipe in the sewage system.

As they were driving away, Isman turned to Gerardo.

"And if she says, 'no'?"

"Well, no problem. We simply install the system somewhere else and leave this. Now, we know we have a safe house."

===

Chapter Forty-nine: A Sentimental Chilean
Santiago, Chile

When Gerardo returned to Santiago, he spent a couple days at home. He was resting and reading up on all the preparations. His work would influence history, as had his uncle's. In the new understanding of history, both would be redeemed. His parents, still in the south, still holding on to the ancient ways of tradition, honor and patriotism would one day see the valor in their son's work toward a new comprehension.

On his third day home, he was reflecting on his actions to come. As his uncle had gotten older, the people forgot the value of living in structure and with self-respect. They came to regard his work as dictatorial, unpopular in a democratic world. His uncle, despite his health and vigor, could therefore not be seen by the world as a figurehead for the new movement. His actions for the benefit of his country were misconstrued and he was therefore vilified. He could not be the visible leader. It was too soon. Even he saw this. But, in the absence of his uncle, an opportunity was created. He sipped his coffee and looked out his window on the city. With the Andes in the background, snow capped and majestic, he knew his efforts were not misplaced. The world needed men of vision and discipline, able to make tough decisions for the benefit of all.

Just at this thought, his doorbell rang.

"Octavio, what a pleasant surprise! To what do I owe the honor?"

Octavio gave a slight bow with a smile and Gerardo invited him in.

"*¿Se puede hablar?*" asked Octavio.

"Yes, it is safe to speak."

"Good. Welcome back. I trust your trip was a success and all is arranged with our pharaonic friends?"

Gerardo nodded.

"I come today to finalize our plans. Everything is set and you and I both know that our work is crucial to the future. Crucial work demands men and women of exceptional ability. History has, time and again, demonstrated the need for prudent decisions and wise counsel."

Gerardo looked at Octavio. What was the old man hinting at?

"For this reason, I have spent the last weeks questioning our decision."

"Oh? Which decision?"

"The decision regarding the boy."

There it is, thought Gerardo. The boy. The old man had taken a liking to the boy. Hadn't they all? He was an interesting young man, so full of promise and energy, willing to learn and do. But the mission was too critical to hesitate for sentiment. That the boy might one day come around was too risky. Had there been different circumstances... well, that was always the case with tough decisions. Different circumstances would negate difficult decisions.

"What are your thoughts?"

"Well," began Octavio, "if our mission is true and just, and this boy is as good as we all believe him to be, then I wonder why we would end his life? Why not detain him, have him watch how the process unfolds. Surely he will come to see the wisdom in our actions. Gerardo, you know what the boy can do. You have seen the initiative to accomplish tasks set before him or even hinted at before him. Why would we waste that?"

Gerardo never doubted Octavio; there was never a reason. Even now, he doubted not. But this silly talk belittled him. He had to end it.

"Octavio, our country was founded by less than two hundred Spaniards fighting off thousands of locals in hostile and foreign terrain. They had to be brave and strong, sure. But, they also had to make decisions. They could not have accomplished Chile without bloodshed. They had to be efficient and consistent to achieve success. Do you think Pedro de Valdivia would have given a gun to a *compadre* who was too weak to pull the trigger?"

"Pedro was a leader of men," replied Octavio. "He needed every man then to win. Without trust in his men, he was nothing."

"And as leader, if he doubted his own decisions and changed them, his men – who so desperately needed it – would have lost their confidence in him."

This was a bold statement for Gerardo. It was the first time he dared to assert his position in the group against one of the founders of the movement not only in Chile, but in all of South America.

Octavio walked over to the window and took out a *cigarillo*. Gerardo walked over, and Octavio offered him one. He lit both.

"*Así es*," he said. "I will make the call. It will be done."

==

Gerardo sighed slightly when Octavio departed. He had played his hand, and Octavio recognized his position. At the parting, the handshake reaffirmed their commitment to each other, and to the cause. Gerardo continued his work, comforted in his trust of Octavio.

==

Octavio left the home of Gerardo and went to a safe phone. He dialed the numbers for his contact in Egypt. "When you take him, take him. Do no harm. He is to be kept alive for information until such time as I personally speak to him. Understood?"

"*Aiwa*" said the man on the other end. "We will take him to the house and wait."

"Good. Be discreet. Tell no one of this. To all else, this matter is settled. I will be in contact."

===

Chapter Fifty: Alicia and JT
Maadi, Cairo

After Alicia sent her sailor off on a six month tour, she focused her energies on JT. In the beginning, she was determined to complete her mission. She found her discussions with JT engaging and felt they sharpened her own arguments. Her efforts were spent on tracking JT's schedule and habits, his skills and interests. Everything about him screamed college kid trying to enjoy the ride.

An average week for JT consisted of hopping on buses to get to class at the American University in Cairo, lunch with some friends, and maybe some pick-up basketball. If there was time, a visit to the computer lab to check e-mail. At the apartment, he and a roommate would head to the fruit and vegetable stand to buy dinner. On Tuesdays and Thursdays, JT went to rugby. There were occasional variances, like boxing or a small trip to the beach.

JT was still used by Gerardo. Packages were sent and JT had to pick-up and deliver them in specified periods of time, or drop them off with Isman. The work was easy and JT felt safe. He actually felt bad at times telling Jason that he had only an envelope to deliver. Beyond their working relationship, his interactions with Jason built the foundation of a good friendship. That is what Alicia saw.

For the most part, his life was as routine as it could get for an American in Cairo who did not speak Arabic. Alicia sent regular reports. Gerardo made sure to read each one. He could not help suppressing a smile that JT was enjoying the experience.

Alicia, too, was smiling watching JT. There was something innocent about him. He took in each experience and seemed to savor it as she could not recall ever doing. Their discussion had her thinking, wondering if maybe through too much of travel and "society" she had become numb to the thrill of exotic adventures. JT's joy in not only attempting new meals, smoking shisha pipes and traveling but also in describing them to Alicia over coffee started to spread to her. She would arrive home afterwards and, when someone asked her what she had been doing, she found herself smiling when she mentioned JT's name.

Towards the end of the semester, the rugby team received an invitation from the HMS Invincible to play a game. The British ship was pulling into port and had 400 sailors ready to run around on the pitch. The men's and women's team would both get games, then the club would host the sailors back at the clubhouse. The men's game itself was close for the first of the three halves. In the second half, the sailors put in 15 new players, which meant fresh legs and pent up energy. By the third half and more new British players on the pitch, the game was over.

Alicia was watching JT on the sideline when one of the British sailors came over to talk to her. The girls had played already, so Alicia knew Mary as the outside center. They chatted for a few moments, then Mary asked about the Cairo Rugby scrum half. Did she know him? What was his name? What was he doing in Egypt?

As Alicia was answering these questions, she knew Mary was sizing him up for a possible flirtation later. She actually felt herself becoming jealous.

When Mary asked if JT was available, Alicia found herself saying, "He's with me." Mary got the hint, and moved right on to the hooker. Alicia talked up Kimani and knew Mary and he would meet later.

JT exited the game after the second half and Alicia walked over and handed him a beer. They talked for a bit and Alicia just kept looking at him.

"What? What are you looking at? Do I have mud in my hair or something?"

"No. You just played a good game, that's all," replied Alicia.

It was not until later at the clubhouse, after a few drinks, that Alicia knew she had to tell JT what she had said to Mary, and why. They were talking in the corner, waiting for the next game of pool.

"Listen, JT, I need to apologize for something."

JT took a sip of beer and looked quizzically at her.

"You see that girl over there talking to Kimani? Well, she was asking about you on the sideline earlier."

"Really? She's cute."

"Yeah, well, I kind of told her that you and I were together."

JT looked at Alicia. Alicia lowered her eyes, to hide her blush. Until that moment, she had not thought to consider whether JT harbored similar feelings.

"I'm sorry, JT. I did not mean to ruin your chances."

"I'm not. And you didn't."

JT picked up her chin, smiled, and kissed her.

In the noise of the clubhouse, no one noticed the two of them kissing.

"Why don't we try to make that statement true?" said JT.

==

For the next few weeks, Alicia and JT spent most of their time together. They went to coffee houses and shows, watched TV and played backgammon, they even took to the Antiquities Museum to just walk and talk in some quiet space.

As the semester was winding down, the two of them started to talk about what would happen between them. Neither wanted to separate. JT, in particular, found himself in a quandary. After Janey, he felt confused and unsure of himself. Mariela was a great memory, and he would never forget her. But he had known that it was temporary. In Egypt, JT was starting to fall for Alicia. She was intelligent and witty, well read and passionate in debates. While he started their time together with the idea it was temporary, he found himself not believing it had to end. His work for both Gerardo and José Luis was to end soon. He could always claim he needed time off. Plus, he convinced himself that his new connections would help him.

Before he was going to ask for help, though, something inside told him he should verify with Alicia that she wanted him to stay with her. It would be a big night; her answer would influence the direction of his life.

==

Alicia, too, was falling for JT. She had never met anyone like him in her life. She was the first of the two to realize how deep her emotions ran. When he asked her to go to dinner on Saturday night, her heart leapt. They had not had a formal dinner together in quite some time. Was he going to declare his love for her? But then doubt crept into her head. JT had less than a month left in Egypt. Was he breaking up with her? Was he going to make a clean break now instead of the last week?

Her mind was further befuddled by the latest directive she received. The need for JT in Egypt was finished. Alicia was to communicate to Isman a convenient and safe situation in which to take JT and remove him from the area.

She felt confused and frightened. Her family knew vaguely of her mission, and now she needed the comfort of her sister, the advice of her sister. She walked into her sister's room, and without details, explained her confusion. Boy trouble, it was nothing new. But Alicia knew that this dinner would be the perfect opportunity for the Society to end her mission. The two of them would be away from observers, away from help and isolated from intervention. If the last directive she received was to be followed, this was the best opportunity.

Sarah and Alicia were very similar in their opinions, at least before Alicia met JT. Sarah believed in the mission and her work and knew her family's efforts were for a greater good. Sarah had been in a similar situation, she explained. She loved a man deeply, but staying with him would have jeopardized her ability to best serve the Society.

"And what did you do?" asked Alicia.

"I trusted in the mission, in the Society. If this man is truly the one, then our mission remains of the utmost importance. When we succeed, he will come to understand why you have acted as you will. It will be clear to him and his love for you will be deeper. If, however, your other fear is realized and he ends your relationship, how will you ever be able to explain that? Is one man worth risking the work we do for God?"

It was a miserable week for Alicia. It was not until the morning of the dinner that she finally contacted Isman. She slipped the message in a container and dropped it down the sink.

As soon as her left hand released it, her right hand went to grab for it. She missed.

===

Chapter Fifty-one: Mission Completed?

Compared to Chile and the work he did there, Egypt was mundane. Of course, he realized that it was anything but commonplace. He had been in constant communication with either Gerardo or José Luis, and was manipulating up to eight different secret codes, methods or "drops". He realized that if Chile was how an agency recruited spies, then Egypt was how the work was actually done. He was uncertain whether he would ever continue in this work, or if he even wanted to do so. It was about time to go home.

At one of the last practices, the boys from the team decided to take JT and Kimani to Deals for one last night of revelry. JT knew he would have to say good-bye to Jason, to let him know that he had no more communiqués to deliver. He also had to find Isman and say farewell to him. He had learned to walk with an eye always scanning for trouble or an ambush. He became secretive about everything, and doubted every word anyone said to him. At the same time, he realized his experiences were unique and might never present themselves again. Appreciating and enjoying people, events and trips in spite of his doubts made the semester a deeper part of who he was. He might not miss the work, but he would miss Jason and Isman, in their own rights.

Isman was the taxi driver to that last practice, and JT told him about dinner Saturday night.

"You will need a ride, yes?" asked Isman. And before JT could answer, "And so I will take you. Free of charge. My way of good-bye. It has been a pleasure to know you and this last chance to wish you well as you have dinner with that pretty lady of yours will be an honor."

It was arranged that Isman would pick him up and then drive him home.

"Unless I don't need a ride home" said JT with a smile.

"Oh, JT, you silly man! Of course, of course, with one look I will leave."

Later that night, JT was saying good-bye to Jason. It was full of male bravado and how they had a great semester. They each spent time recalling good plays from the rugby pitch, and laughing about some of the antics at the clubhouse.

"Seriously, Jason, I want to thank you."

It was late and there were just a few guys remaining at the bar. Kimani was hanging out with some of the other guys, laughing about the semester.

"I don't know how I would have kept sane without you. Knowing that a Marine had my back was very reassuring, even if the work was boring."

"Never say the work is boring; that is when you let your guard down and are susceptible to an enemy."

"Always the Marine, eh?"

"That's right, JT. And I had a great time getting to know you, too. I'm guessing that since you're leaving, you're done your work? Mission accomplished?"

"Semester's over, man!" said JT, but he was thinking about that. Was the mission accomplished? Did he do enough to help José Luis stop whatever it is the Gerardo and his cohorts actually were planning on doing?

JT did not sleep that night. His head swirled around the last year of his life, from Dean Bulgiuno to Janey, to the embassy party to Octavio and Gerardo. Never in his life did he picture living in Chile and Egypt, meeting los Cotarín or even Isman. Or Alicia.

==

On Saturday, JT was clear. He knew he wanted to stay with Alicia. He called the restaurant to confirm reservations and to reserve a couple bottles of wine.

Alicia was frantic on Saturday. What was JT going to say? How would she react? Had she done the right thing by sending that message?

When she pulled up to the restaurant, she saw Isman outside. JT was already inside. She walked in and smiled. JT was wearing a shirt and tie, had a table with a bottle of wine and a candle.

"Hey beautiful, how are you tonight?" asked JT.

"Better, now that I see you."

They sat down and JT poured the wine. He had it all planned out. He was going to pass some idle chatter, reminisce about the semester and their time together, and then, right before dessert, profess his feelings for her and gauge her response. It was not until she walked in, however, that he realized with clarity how he felt. He knew. And he knew he had to follow his plan or risk sound liking a lunatic.

But he could not stop himself.

"Alicia, the thing is, my time here... the semester... meeting you..."

"Whoa, hey, settle down. Slow down. Take a

breath and start over."

She took her own deep breath.

"Alicia, I love you and I don't want to leave you."

"Oh, JT, me neither" she gushed and grabbed his hand.

"I'll do whatever I can to stay with you. I'll transfer colleges. I'll move to Cairo or England or wherever you want to live. Meeting you has changed my life."

Alicia had tears in her eyes, and her lip was quivering.

"I love you, too, JT, and I would do all that for you. I just don't want to lose you."

They sat there holding hands. JT was glowing with joy, and Alicia was trembling. Would she have to tell him she had planned to betray him? That she did betray him!?

"Well, then, let's figure out what we need to do." said JT.

Alicia wiped her eyes and looked at JT.

"Just let me get some air."

"You okay?"

"Of course, but with the tears, I just, I just need some air on my face. I'll be back in a minute. Have some wine and I'll be right back."

Alicia walked out front and looked for Isman. She had to stop him. JT was no threat to the Society or to Gerardo. If she had to do so, she'd quit the Society. But Isman was nowhere to be seen. And his cab was gone. She sighed, tonight was not the night. She still had time to fix this and be with JT.

She composed herself and walked back into the restaurant.

But JT was gone.

===

Chapter Fifty-two: A Package from Janey

After her meeting with Dr. Ogilvie, Janey tried to follow his advice. At first, she rarely did anything but class and work. Eventually, her friends convinced her to do a "girls' night". She had fun. Then she was talked into playing intra-mural volleyball, and she had fun again. Over time, she was more active and getting back to her old form. In the beginning, she refused every advance from a guy. But, after a couple months and some cajoling from her friends, she went on some casual coffee dates. She never really planned for anything to happen. It was just a way to pass the time. In her mind, it made clear why she loved JT. None of the dates compared to JT, and despite her friends' opinion that she was putting JT on an impossibly high pedestal, she never made it past a couple dates with a guy.

She was very much anticipating JT's return. She had an idea that it would take time to convince him she never stopped loving him, and if she had to do so, she would introduce him to TJ and he could tell the story, too. When he did not show up after Chile, she was confused and angry. Dr. Ogilvie had not mentioned his staying longer in Chile. Calls to his office went unanswered. She started to write him letters, hoping and pleading for information. She only received vague, non-committal responses.

Chris Grelsh never revealed to Janey any information. As much as it pained him, he figured it was better for her to move on. After receiving the Fed Ex package from Janey, he was getting ready to call it a night. JT had gone missing, Alicia had gone missing, and there were no leads. Sipping that whiskey and staring at the package got to him. He had grown fond of JT in an almost big brother fashion. JT was his responsibility; he was in Grelsh's care. The package was sitting on his desk and he needed to open it. He nearly fainted when he opened the letter and saw the contents. JT was alive!

For the first couple pages, the information mostly filled in the gaps of what had happened to him. From what Chris could gather, JT was stuck in some hell hole of a house in the desert. For whatever reason, Gerardo or someone had kept him alive. JT's notes were short, nothing but facts. He was in some abandoned town, about twenty guards, and there was a little shepherd boy helping him.

Grelsh's mind was racing. Their surveillance of Ireland in May had yielded little worthwhile information. Whatever plans the MacNessa had made, they were done exceptionally well and nearly beyond tracking. From time to time, one of the telecommunications experts would claim to hear a secret code. No one could crack it. The best the agents Grelsh had in place could do was spot an occasional suspect leaving the country. There was little apparent rhyme or reason as to modes or times: some left at dawn on a flight, others at night on the trains, others midday on the ferry across the channel to France. For three weeks after the meeting date (or at least the date they supposed) suspects were still seen leaving the country. It made no sense, to any of the agents. And Grelsh's boss was fuming. He had a Senate Sub-Committee meeting in a day and without answers as to what value their mission had, all their careers were over.

Reading this, Grelsh was only thinking of how to use it to find JT. While he had not written off the assignment, the chance to find this kid re-kindled his spirit. He was going through the pages quickly, almost too quickly, when his eyes caught a double underline.

After he was taken from the restaurant by two men, JT was thrown into the back of a cab, hooded and gagged. He recognized the one captor as Isman, and he was furious. The men were speaking excitedly and without concern in Arabic. Surveillance had shown that JT never took classes and never learned more than the random greeting or directions. JT, however, had a teacher no one knew about. While the plane trip had introduced him covertly to Arabic and he was able to pick some up on his own, it was his daily visit to the fruit stand that was of greatest importance. The vendor was a kindly man who recognized on his first visit to buy fruit that JT spoke little to no Arabic. Day by day, he taught JT how to say fruits, then numbers, then quantities, then greetings; each day JT became more comfortable with Arabic. Now, in the back seat of the cab, he understood every word they said. It was Gerardo who wanted him taken, but Octavio wanted him to live. The grab had to be done before the May meeting, and he was to be held until the end of July, when Octavio would personally come to see the boy.

"But why would he come here, to the desert, instead of straight back to Chile? That makes no sense."

"Bah," said Isman, "what do you know? He comes here to see this American. He likes him, I think. Besides, coming here is not simply to see him. He will be on his way back to Chile. After the meeting in May, he spent time confirming information in Europe and Asia. He will stop here on his way back. Don't you see? He has to be back in Chile before the festival in August. He will stop here, do what he has to do, and then be back in time for the signal. And then, my friend, you and I will be rewarded for our faithful service."

Grelsh read the facts: festival in August, all members back to their countries to await a signal. That was it, August. They had less than two months to prepare for a strike. Was that enough time?

He rushed to the office of John Maloney.

===

Chapter Fifty-three: Final Journeys

The meeting in May in County Donegal, Ireland had been an unmitigated success. James Sr. left the hospital long enough to attend and show his face. Every member arrived unscathed and without being followed.

James Sr. set up the ring ceremony in the beginning so that everyone would know to whom to look. Jr. was now the official leader of the Society, the direct descendent of Saer. The room was silent as the mists of Ireland while the ceremony concluded. Each of the delegates knew the purpose of their work and each held a deeply personal commitment to their cause. For them, this was God's work.

With the ring on his finger, Jr. felt a fire burn within him. His whole life had been building to this moment. James Sr. stepped to the side as he felt his own fire dwindle.

Jr. knew it was time, time to inspire his men and women, time to look each of them in the eyes and transfer his confidence and his trust.

"Gentlemen, ladies, friends and family, I greet you in the name of our Lord, God, and thank you for your dedication, your support and your faith. You truly are the chosen peoples of God to carry forth his message like the Flood to baptize the world anew!

Each of us, in our own countries, in our cultures, in our language and in our Ibrahamic belief, has seen the work of man when he is separate from God. We know through experience the evil which man and woman can commit. That is the easy part. Greed, jealousy, idolatry, has not God communicated to us the effects of sin? Did not Moses, Confucius, Mohammed and Jesus all try to teach our fellow man the effects of choosing the poor path? And yet what has happened time and again throughout our common history? Our brothers have fought their brothers, our sisters have betrayed our sisters, and our religious leaders – from the Pope to the imam to the rabbi to the Confucian king – have encouraged them to do so... in the name of God! Whose God, I ask? Your God? My God? My God wants no such thing! Your God wants no such thing!

God wants us to make wise choices, to learn from our history and our mistakes, to communicate and celebrate and love each other! We have Free Will; yes, of course we do. You are all here because you exercised your Free Will and have embraced the Lord and His work here on Earth. We are here because Noah embraced the word of the Lord and Saer embraced the word of the Lord and Ferceirtne embraced the Lord. At a time when women were property, the Lord inspired Ferceirtne to trust his daughter to lead. At a time when people killed each other as pagans, the Lord had our forefathers travel and mingle and come to learn and love one another, as He loves us!

I ask you: do the actions of man reflect the actions we have seen our God do? Do the actions of man honor the God of us all? Do the actions of man fill you with joy knowing that on the Day of Judgment you have to explain that, as your brother's keeper, you have failed? You have failed to assist, failed to correct, failed to love your brother through inaction? Through lethargy? Through fear? I have no fear save that of God, Himself. Do you have fear?

In your hearts, what do you know? I'll tell you what I know. I know I love. I love God. I love you all, here. I love each man, woman and child I see. And I know it breaks my heart when I learn of an error made which does dishonor to God. I know it pains me when I learn that my inaction had contributed in some way to that dishonor. Why did God send Jesus? Why did God send Mohammed? Why did God send his servant Ghandi? They were examples. We are to stand up for that which we believe, in the face of the Roman legions or the Arab princes or even the might of another British Empire.

My brothers and sisters, we are not gods. We are not sent from heaven as angels of mercy or doom. We are humble servants; we are humble servants sent to fight for God. To fight for His wisdom above our own human failings and beyond our petty squabbles of land, money and power.

We are few; in the face of six billion people, we are few. But so, too, were the Greeks at Thermopylae. A small band of three hundred held back and advanced in the face of two hundred thousand. And why? It was because they chose the battle place, they chose the method. They had superior methods and tactics, they had determined leaders and they each, to a man, believed in their cause and would not be turned from it!

We will not be turned from our cause, for our cause is the cause of the Creator, of the God of us all. We are His Moses leading His people out of the bondage of humanistic and relativistic slavery! We are His Noah offering an Ark to the people in the

Flood of sin. We are His Joan of Arc defending the Kingdom of Heaven!

As we tighten our bonds, we grasp each others' hands and know that we are in the struggle for the soul of humanity. The hand you clasp depends as much on you as you on it. We are one body moving forward. We are one mind moving forward. We are one spirit burning in the glory and honor of God!

At the festival, I will proclaim the glory of God and the world will come to know through each of us how God will come again to welcome us into his Sanctuary to save us from that greatest of punishments, the absence of His presence.

We fight on and on in the name of God and we trust in His divine providence and grace."

Tears streaming down their faces, hands clenched and chests swelled, the group bellowed out in unison, "AMEN!"

===

Chapter Fifty-four: The Phone Call

John Maloney was skeptical at first. Who wouldn't be? It sounded preposterous: a *coup d'etat* in various countries at the same time in order to establish a worldwide ruling elite? Grelsh was ready for this, however, and knew exactly what to say, how to say it, and with what urgency. Maloney came to believe, and set Grelsh on track to stop it, with whatever resources he needed. The heads of every intelligence agency in the United States were brought to a meeting and debriefed. They, in turn, had to take that info and fly to every country they could to inform their counterparts of the plan. Logistically, it was a nightmare. Pragmatically, in the world of intelligence and misinformation, it was near impossible to be able to trust others with such classified information. There had to be a rapid, but very thorough, vetting out process of who could and would be trusted and which actions to recommend. Worse, at least politically, the presidents and prime ministers and kings and queens had to be left out of the information loop, at least for now. They could not afford a public opinion poll dictating a decision of this magnitude.

After the meeting, Maloney's biggest mental block was who was involved. Grelsh explained the code they heard before the May meeting.

"We can't crack it? What the hell do we pay code breakers for, then?!" he demanded.

One of the code breakers had pulled Grelsh aside and explained his thoughts that this was not a code, *per se*.

"He called it the Navajo Code, sir."

"Keep talking, Chris."

Grelsh reminded Maloney of the Navajos used by the US military during World War II due to the nature of their language and the difficulty in comprehension. One of the biggest obstacles to deciphering it was not the code, but the language. This breaker's idea to Grelsh was that this was not a code, but some language no one has ever heard of before. They had linguists try to track it, but they had no luck whatsoever in finding roots or morphisms of words.

"So what do we do, then, Chris? Just keep trying to break it, gather up every linguist in the country and offer them a million dollars to break it?"

"No, sir, we don't. We can't crack this, at least not in time. I think we need to keep monitoring calls and communications, build up a vocabulary bank of some sort. Any time anyone in the world uses one of these words, we have them tracked. For the ten people we know of currently, we have eight of them being followed. I know, sir, that will be a lot of manpower. But, because we can use regular agents, we do not yet have to explain why they are tracking these people. Just tell them to do their job."

Maloney rubbed his eyes. "When does this all go down?"

"Sometime in August. Using what we know from our information and from what we can infer about the organization, there is a festival in August in Ireland called Lughnasa. There is a deep cultural tradition there. In ancient Ireland, it was a time to celebrate and anoint new high kings. Again, given our intel, it fits."

Maloney stood up and looked at Grelsh in the eyes.

"Sir, we have agents mobile now. Honestly, sir, people are responding to our call with energy and zeal. They don't know what's going on, but they can infer that so much action means something big is on the horizon, and they all want to be a part of it. We can do this. We are trained for this."

Maloney turned around and picked up the phone.

"Mr. President, you need to hear this."

===

Chapter Fifty-five: Truth be Told

After his speech, the men and women of the Society celebrated with a grand dinner, musicians, storytellers, poets and dancing. This was the big send off to bring to fruition their lives' work, as well as the work of generations of their ancestors. Each and every member knew the history of the Society and of the MacNessa family. The mission inspired them, burned in their hearts and guided their every thought, action and deed. Not the least of those so affected was James Jr.

He finished the speech and swelling in his heart and in his mind was not pride, but joy. He saw himself not as a prophet or some kind of "chosen" one; he saw himself and his compatriots as tools of God. Simply to be used by God, to be touched by His Grace, was humbling and energizing simultaneously.

The next couple of weeks were spent in logistics and final planning. Communications systems were triple checked, travel arrangements and alternative means of travel were verified. After millennia of preparation and anticipation, a few more weeks to finalize details were nothing.

Ten days after the meeting, James Jr. came into his father's office to ask some advice. As he entered, he noticed his father, slumped over his desk. He rushed in screaming, yelling for someone to call for help. When help arrived, they were able to resuscitate him on the way to the hospital. Jr. rode in the ambulance.

James Sr. lay in a coma for a week. Jr. ran his work again out of an adjacent room, spending every night asleep at his father's bedside in a chair.

On the day he awoke, the doctor pulled Jr. aside.

"James, how you doing?"

"I'm fine, doc, just fine. What's going on with my da?"

The doctor walked over to the couch and motioned for Jr. to sit down.

"James, this is your father's second heart attack. By running some tests, we have been able to determine that your father's had cardiac problems for years. He's lucky to have lived this long. Had we been able to perform diagnostics before, run some basic physicals, we could have caught it, and properly treated him."

Jr. looked at the doctor.

"And?"

"And, your father never came in for tests. His father had heart problems, I'm presuming his father's father had heart problems. But without the tests, there was no way for us to proffer a diagnosis. Now that he's here, it does not look good. He's awake now, but he may lapse into a coma tonight. If he lapses, he may never come out of it. I'm sorry, James. I'm truly sorry."

The doctor patted Jr.'s hand, squeezed, and left him alone.

An elephant was sitting on Jr.'s chest. Everything, their work, their hopes, their dreams... their mission! The father was probably never going to see it. Could he tell him that? How? Did he already know? Did the Sr. already know that his time had come?

Jr. paced the halls for quite some time before re-entering his father's room. Upon entering, the father rolled over.

"Son?"

"Yeah, da, it's me. Go back to sleep. I'll be here."

"No, no, I was waiting for you."

Indeed, he had. He did know. He could tell from the pain of this attack that the end was near. When he awoke in the hospital, he was, frankly, amazed to be alive.

"It's time, son. It's time."

"I know, da. I know. We're on the threshold of completing our mission."

"No, son, that's not what I mean."

Jr. looked quizzically at his father as he inhaled one deep, long breath.

"Son, what I am about to tell you has been passed down for generations of MacNessa's, from father to child in absolute secrecy. No one, not a wife, not a sibling, not a pet, no other than a father and the chosen child has ever heard these words. They are a deathbed confessional.

After the Norman invasion of Ireland, Laurence MacNessa maintained cordial relations with the Normans. He was one of the few to accept quickly that hatred of the English would not drive them from the land. In order to move forward, one had to work with the situation. As a result, he became rich and prosperous. All the while, he never forgot his Irish identity, nor did he abandon his culture, his music or his religion. In those times, that was a curiosity. People began to wonder, how did he do it? Was he a devil? Was he a druid?

Slowly, over time, other leading families began to regain some of the traditional riches, lands and honor. These families were shrewd, and they had to be. Failure to appease the Normans could mean a new English garrison stationed in their manors. But, failure to please the people could mean a fire.

These families stayed together. They went into business together, they attended church services together, they sang in the drinking holes together and they dined in Norman estates together."

Sr. took a breath, and Jr. passed him a glass of water. Jr.'s attention to his father's story was as it ever was, rapt and focused. His father knew this, and was grateful he would only have to tell this story the one time. He was struggling. The emotional toll of telling this was weakening his system. His blood pressure, his heart, everything was losing strength, but he knew he had to finish this story, even if the last word was his dying breath.

"As you may have guessed, these families are those Irish who are, in our Society, of Gaelic ancestry. But, as you are aware, there are those with Norman last names. These families are both entrants into the Society. Remember the methods of Ferceirtne, our very own methods to this day! They functioned well then as they do now. Those Gaelic and Norman families bonded and forged ahead together, advancing the mission of the Society."

James Sr. continued to describe the advances of the Society through Ireland and beyond; the locations of great families and their stores of information, supplies; the pivotal moments in the history of the Society. In fact, these were all things known to James Jr. He was a bit confused, unsure of where his father was going with his story. His father was a step ahead.

"Son, you know the methods, you know the strategies, the partners, the pressure points, the hopes and aspirations of the Society. You trust, as I did, in the mission and you trust that through its purity all its handiwork is purified. For that purpose, you are worthy to wear the ring which is not worthy to be worn."

"Da, are you okay? You rambling here?"

"Son, listen."

James Sr.'s eyes welled with tears, his chest was heaving with sobs, and his body was trembling. Jr. was about to call for a nurse, when his father grabbed his arm.

"Son, you need to know this. My father told me this on his own deathbed, as I tell you this from my deathbed. This which I am about to tell you holds the power to make or break our mission. Over the last thousand years, our ancestors have deepened their devotion to the mission and their faith in God through the Society. Now, you wonder why I told you all about Laurence MacNessa. You wonder why I focus on him as if he is the starting point; why I explain to you again how he rose in prominence, raised his neighbors and somehow remained secure from the surrounding troubles of the Irish countryside. You wonder why I recounted the documents and the history of the Society. I tell you this now, I must tell you this now, in it entirety, because it is all based on the lie, the false story, that Laurence MacNessa told the Norman invaders."

Jr. let go of his father's hand and his head shook, slightly but with a jolt.

"Laurence did see the coming of the Normans and did recognize that to hate them would do nothing but impoverish him and his. To secure himself, and to secure his kinfolk, he created this elaborate tale of Saer. He recruited a few key people, they forged documents and stories, created fake medallions, seals, codes and rituals out of thin air. They created MacNessa."

Both James' were heaving, trying to catch their breath.

"Son, our Society was born out of a lie, but we have carried it forth in true spirit. As my father had done, as his father had done. We have carried on the Society for the right purpose, for the true mission."

Jr. was pacing the room, shaking his head in disbelief, unable to look at his father who was trying to sit up, to press his tale.

"Only you know this secret, son. Only you can decide the fate of the Society and our life's work. We may be created from a lie, but we have worked toward…, and as my father trusted me, I trust you to continue to work toward, the…"

Jr. walked out of the room and never heard the last word his father said.

Sr. breathed out his last breath and never finished the word.

===

Chapter Fifty-six: JT

JT's existence was rather routine in the desert. He had long since lost hope of rescue. In the beginning weeks after sending the package off, his mind oscillated between fear that it never made it to her and expectation that she would walk up to the house to free him. That hope, that possibility that Janey would be the one to walk up and free him was powerful. He felt energized. He felt that his efforts would have been recognized. For a bit, he also thought he still loved her.

JT told the Bedouin boy that Janey had been his one and only love, that he should have left this life behind for her. That was mostly true. He often times wondered what would have happened had he not come to Egypt. In fact, still being alive in the desert after so much time had him wondering if Gerardo was actually a part of anything other than his business. If he had gone home, would they have worked it out? Would he have been able to do so? Had both of them changed too much?

He had a great quantity of time to think as a prisoner; the boy could not be his constant companion, after all. He had loved Janey, that was true. He still smiled at some of the memories. But his true love, the one that still burned in his heart hotter than the desert sun, was Alicia. He knew he could not mention her to the boy. That would endanger her and her family in Cairo. For JT, one of the few ideas that made him chuckle out loud was the realization that he was planning on leaving this life behind for Alicia. He was simply one day late.

JT continued to talk to the boy. While he never mentioned Alicia, his descriptions of the girl he loved were descriptions of Alicia: her hair, her smell, her lips and her smile. The boy stared in wonder as JT described looking into the starry night and seeing her eyes.

Beyond the love interest of the boy, JT found a bright, inquisitive mind. They each pestered the other with questions. Geography, history, religion, wildlife, diets and friends were all topics of discussion. It was a great time for both of them. Then, it just stopped. JT could not see what had happened, but after leaving one day, the boy was yelled at by someone. JT heard scraping of shoes on the sand and gravel and assumed it was the boy. He could only pray that nothing would happen to him.

JT learned the layout of the area around them, and piece by piece even was able to approximate his location on a mental map. The energy of talking to the boy faded over time. His mind slowly lost focus. The guards visited him less often, which meant he received less food, less water. He was thin, scraggly haired and bearded, dirty and smelly. His teeth hurt, his eyes hurt, even skin was becoming tender. His bodily functions were so depleted he barely needed the slop bucket afforded him. Once in a while, in moments of prolonged isolation, he rattled the door or tried to kick the bars on the windows; the futile efforts of a tired prisoner.

At various points, to try remaining sane, he would recite stories, or poems, go through movie plots he remembered, highlight some of the better memories he had or even go through vocabulary, either Spanish or Arabic. Thus, each of the few scattered items about him had several names.

It must have been a month or so, he reckoned, since the boy last visited. It was nearly noon, and he had not seen any guard, or heard any voices, for a couple days. He was hungry, weak and thirsty. Outside, a random bird came to alight. JT propped himself in the chair, wrapped his arms around the bars, and watched. The bird started to sing, and JT closed his eyes. He smiled. It was calm, it was peaceful. He was even in the shade.

The bird whistled its tune for but a few minutes, which JT mistook for hours. Suddenly, it flew off. JT stirred, mostly to try to listen. He heard a sound, but it was not the chirping. There was more scraping of feet. With his memory gone, he thought he was hearing the scraping of the boy's feet being dragged away. He quizzically murmured the boy's name. As he noticed the sound coming closer, however, he opened his eyes to see. He could make out men, with guns, circling in on his location.

He was too weak to fight, too weak to scream, too weak to care.

At least the bird was pretty, thought JT closing his eyes again, just as the first soldier opened the door with his weapon drawn, and noticed the slumped American in the chair.

JT had been waiting for this moment; he knew he was going to die. He was just waiting to hear the word from the leader, that simple twist of the tongue which would mean his death and the end of his mission.

===

Epilogue

Everything contained in this manuscript is based on fact. I have gathered the information from Janey, an agent in the National Security Agency, and other sources. There is a secret coup to overthrow our traditional world governments with a new form heretofore never seen in practice. What you are just read will probably leave you doubting and incredulous. It did so for me.

I did not believe it when my friend told it to me. Even after she showed me the papers, I could not, would not believe. But, then she went missing. I have not seen Janey in several months; her husband was arrested; and her lawyer was found dead in an "accidental" car crash.

Now I believe. Getting the word out is the only thing I know to do.

Bill Hoehn

Special Agent, FBI

Glossary of Foreign Language Vocabulary

Chapter Two:
Ink
1. Fil beyt (Arabic)   - In the house

Chapter Three:
The Recruit
1. Apellido (Spanish)   - Last name

Chapter Seven:
The Last RSVP
1. Ya venimos. (Spanish)   - We are already coming.
2. Está listo. (Spanish)   - It is ready.
3. Ciao. (Spanish)   - Goodbye.

Chapter Twelve:
A New San Martín
1. Mi sobrino (Spanish)   - My nephew
2. Eso es. (Spanish)   - That is it.
3. Nuestros hermanos   – Our Puerto Rican
   puertorriqueños   brothers / siblings
   (Spanish)

Chapter Fourteen:
¡Bienvenidos!
1. Mestizos (Spanish)   - people of mixed
                                              American Indian and
                                              Spanish ancestry

Chapter Fifteen:
Los Cotarín
1. yo poder llevar las   – I can carry my own
   maletas de yo. (Broken   bags.
   Spanish)

2. No, m'ijo, está bien, te
las llevo. Cálmate.
¡Bienvenidos a Chile

\- No, my child, it is okay,
I will carry them
for you. Calm yourself.
Welcome to Chile!

3. Fútbol (Spanish)
\- Soccer
4. La Universidad de Chile
(Spanish)
\- The University of Chile
5. ¿Cachai? (Chilean
Spanish Slang)
\- Get it?
6. Sípo. (Chilean Spanish
Slang)
\- Yes.

Chapter Sixteen:
An Internship
1. Todo. Dime todo.
(Spanish)

\- Everything. Tell me
everything.

Chapter Eighteen:
JT's First Contact
1. ¿Es bueno? (Spanish)
\- Is it good?
2. Sí, sí, es bueno.
(Spanish)
\- Yes, yes, it is good.
3. Buenos días. (Spanish)
\- Good day.
4. Gracias. (Spanish)
\- Thank you.
5. Adiós. (Spanish)
\- Goodbye.
6. Señor (Spanish)
\- Polite greeting to man,
akin to "sir".

7. ¿Cómo está Ud. hoy día?
(Spanish)
– How are you today?

8. Hola. (Spanish)
\- Hello.
9. Super-bien (Spanish)
\- Super well.
10. Un café negro (Spanish)
\- Black coffee
11. Pesos (Spanish)
\- Unit of money similar
to US pennies

Chapter Nineteen:
The Embassy Party
1. Buenas noches (Spanish)   - Good evening.

Chapter Twenty:
The Prince's Calling
1. Táin Bo Cuailgne (Irish)   - The Cattle Raid of
                                  Cooley, Ancient Irish
                                  Epic

Chapter Twenty-two:
JT's Schedule
1. ¿De acuerdo? (Spanish)   - Do we agree?
2. Museo de Arte pre-   - Museum of Pre-
    Columbiano (Spanish)   Columbian Art
3. Mi guapito (Spanish)   - My cute man
                                (affectionate)
4. Mi cafecita (Spanish)   - My coffee girl
                                (affectionate)
5. Hasta mañana (Spanish)   - Until tomorrow

Chapter Twenty-three:
When we are finished...
1. ¿Y? (Spanish)   - And?
2. Es increíble (Spanish)   - It is incredible.
3. Buénopo (Chilean   - Good
    Spanish Slang)   .
4. Bien hecho (Spanish)   - Well done.
5. Tío (Spanish)   - Uncle

Chapter Twenty-six:
The Secret is Out

1. Pisco (Spanish) — Liquor local to Chile and Peru

2. Mi amigo (Spanish) — My friend
3. País (Spanish) — Country
4. Te hablo por cariño (Spanish) — I speak to you out of affection.
5. Y tú (Spanish) — And you
6. Claro (Spanish) — Clearly, of course
7. América del Sur (Spanish) — South America
8. Vecinos sudamericanos (Spanish) — South American neighbors
9. Pues (Spanish) — Well (hesitation word)
10. Nuestro discurso (Spanish) — Our conversation, discussion
11. Mi poeta (Spanish) — My poet
12. Gringo (Spanish) — Spanish slang for US Citizen
13. Odas (Spanish) — Odes, Poetry
14. Oda a la Tempestad (Spanish) — Ode to the Storm
15. Hispanoparlante (Spanish) — Spanish speaker
16. El Como Como (Spanish) — Play on word "como" in Spanish: *The How I Eat*
17. Me muero (Spanish) — I am dying
18. Y no sé por qué — I do not know why.

Chapter Thirty:
Details of the Meeting

1. Coup d'etat (French) — Overthrow of the government; revolt

2. Chicha (Chilean Spanish) — Chilean alcohol, in the wine family

Chapter Thirty-two:
The Semester Ends

1. Me gusta baila baila (Spanish) — I like to dance dance

2. ¿Está bien? (Spanish) — Is that acceptable? (contextual)

3. ¿Cómo están Uds.? (Spanish) — How are you all?

4. Tío (Spanish) — Uncle

Chapter Thirty-three:
Gerardo Bids JT Farewell

1. Vaya con Dios. (Spanish) — Go with God.

Chapter Thirty-six: Egypt Awaits

1. Shukran (Arabic) — Thank-you

Chapter Thirty-seven:
... it is a shame.

1. ¡Qué lástima! (Spanish) — What a shame!